Out of the Shadows

BY

SARAH SINGLETON

Clarion Books

New York

For Fuchia

～～～～～～～

Clarion Books
an imprint of Houghton Mifflin Harcourt Publishing Company
215 Park Avenue South, New York, NY 10003
Copyright © 2006 by Sarah Singleton
Adapted from *Heretic,* first published in Great Britain in 2006
by Simon & Schuster UK Ltd. A Viacom company.
First American edition, 2008.

The text was set in 13-point Loire.

www.clarionbooks.com

Printed in the U.S.A.

Library of Congress Cataloging-in-Publication Data
Singleton, Sarah, 1966–
Out of the shadows / by Sarah Singleton.
p. cm.
Summary: In 1586 England, Elizabeth, whose family is hiding a Catholic priest from
Protestant persecutors, and Isabella, a girl of her own age who was similarly sheltered
by "faerie" folk 300 years earlier when Catholics accused Isabella's mother of
witchcraft, work together to keep the persecutors away.
ISBN: 978-0-618-92722-7
[1. Persecution—Fiction. 2. Reformation—Fiction. 3. Fairies—Fiction.
4. Great Britain—History—Elizabeth, 1558-1603—Fiction.
5. Great Britain—History—Henry III, 1216-1272—Fiction.] I. Title
PZ7.S6178 Out 2008
[Fic]—22
2008010479

MP 10 9 8 7 6 5 4 3 2

Contents

1

The Awakening

Pale November light gleamed through wet black branches. Among the dark stripes of tree trunks, the last autumn leaves were glimmers of gold. The rain had passed, but the forest still dripped.

Curled in the hollow trunk of an elderly oak, the child was half awake, half asleep. The tree was open at the top, like a tall cup, the child lying like the dregs of a drink at the bottom.

The forest poked cold fingers into the child's dreams—the sound of birds in the treetops, the perfume of damp wood and rotting leaves.

At last the child turned in its sleep. It hadn't moved for a very long time—so long that strands of ivy had grown down into the long cup of the hollow trunk and right over the child's body. Now the child tugged at the tough cords with its hands, but the ivy was tight and left thin red marks on its skin.

The child was still dreaming of the other place—the shadow land with its circles of stones and bright fires and its tall crow people dressed in green and gold and black. They weren't always kind, these people. They spoke in deep, cold voices and wore thick bracelets above long white hands. Jewels burned on their necklaces and rings. The child didn't belong with them, and yet it didn't want them to leave. They had something that wasn't theirs, and the child wanted it back. But they drew away, taking the shadow land with them like a sea tide ebbing, leaving the child high and dry—stranded in the forest.

If someone had peered into the tree trunk while the child was in the shadow land, what would he have seen? A heap of dried leaves, perhaps, shaped like a figure, and underneath, a dry bone or two—the link holding the child to the ordinary world. Now that the child had left the shadow land, its body had emerged and formed itself again around the bones and dust of its earthly remains.

The child turned, scratching at the ivy. A crow landed on the oak tree. The wind ruffled its feathers. Spotting the creature inside the trunk, the bird considered, head tipped to the side. It hopped from one lip of the tree cup to the other. Then it flapped black silken wings and gave a single rough call. The sound echoed in the hollow of the tree, and the child opened its eyes.

Nothing made sense at first. The round of light above was broken up by the shape of the bird. The child struggled out of the ivy ropes and sat up. It straightened its fingers and then rubbed its hands over its face, struggling to gather fragments of self together after so long in the shadow land. The body moved of its own accord, but memories were scattered. *Who am I? Where? How?* It was frightening not to know these things, like standing at the edge of a cliff with nothing to hold on to.

Don't be afraid, the child reassured itself. *Wait a while. You'll remember.*

The child broke free of the last strands of ivy and stood up. A litter of leaves fell away, strays that had drifted into the tree. The bird, alarmed by these developments, flew off.

Although the child could not remember who it was, climbing out of the tree was not a problem. The inside of the oak was rough, and woody knobs provided convenient steps. The child's feet were bare and flexible. It reached the top and climbed out, to see the forest from a viewpoint some twelve feet up. Trees spread away in every direction. The sky, through a gauze of bare twigs, was dull gray. A huge fungus, mottled like a toad, clung to the broken bark by the child's right hand.

What to do now? The child clambered down the tree to the ground, sniffed the air, and set off. Walking upright was too difficult. Perhaps the muscles and ligaments of its legs had shortened. So with a stoop it half walked, half ran, using its hands to help itself along.

The forest hadn't changed, except in the detail. The generality of trees and undergrowth, the colors of the autumn season, were just as before. But many individual trees had altered—new grown or gone or split in storms.

Not far from the oak tree, the child halted and tried to stand up straight. But the effort failed and it went on, clambering over fallen branches, ignoring the scratches of brambles. Ahead was a hermitage, its brown stone walls standing among the trees. The child remembered this. It was a holy place, a tiny hut that was home to an old man who was named . . . who was named . . . Jerome. How inviting and welcoming it looked. The child hurried, out of breath now. Then it skidded to a halt.

The hut was a ruin, the thatched roof partly fallen in, the door ripped away. The child hesitated, afraid to look any further. A picture rose in its mind: an archway where a statue stood above a pool of water and a bubbling spring. Now the statue was gone, and the arch was broken. Chunks of stone, half buried by leaves, lay all around the little clearing.

The child began to shiver. Panic rose like a flock of dark birds flapping about in its head.

Who am I?

The child scurried into the ruined cell, a bare room with one window. Not a scrap of furniture remained. No ash in the fireplace. The child ran around the room like a trapped animal. Then it stopped and banged its head on the wall, once, twice, trying to force a memory, wanting to remember. But it hurt very much. The pain stopped the birds flapping in the child's head, but blood trickled down its forehead. In a daze it stumbled out of the hermit's cell to the spring. It dipped fingers into the chilly pool and dabbed water onto the wound. The sun broke through the cloud and spilled light into the clearing. The child leaned over the pool, startled by its own reflection.

What did it see? Long, long hair fell over its shoulders. Skin was stained green and brown from the long years of fallen leaves, ivy, moss. A child? Not really a child anymore. Something else.

It searched its face, looking for clues. *Who am I? Where do*

I belong? It strained to remember, beating at its head with the palms of its hands. It threw itself on the ground and thrashed its arms and legs in a desperate blind panic. The inside of its head seemed to burn up in a storm of black and red, and the outside world disappeared altogether.

Then—a snap. Someone had trodden on a twig close by!

The child froze. It lay still on the ground in sudden terror. Who was coming? Often in the past the child had needed to hide. The hermit, Jerome, had been the only one to be trusted. So the child lay still, listening intently. A minute passed, and another. Perhaps it was safe. The child's heart beat fast. It waited another minute in the cold bed of leaves. All was quiet.

Cautiously, the child lifted its head, looking for the intruder. It crept to its feet, snuffed the air. It turned back to the spring and the broken shrine—and looked directly into the eyes of another human being.

A girl! Yes, a girl. The child held its breath.

They stared at each other—wide-eyed, face to face—just a few feet apart. The girl's mouth dropped open.

The wind rose in the trees. Moments passed. The child's impulse to run wrestled with its desire to ask for help. What to do? How long would they stay like this, just looking at each other?

The child moved first, fear winning out. It shrank back, bunching fists, preparing to flee. But the girl dropped her basket and held out her hand.

"No, wait," she said. "Don't go. I won't hurt you."

The child paused, considering the girl. It knew it should run away and hide. But the sound of her voice was sweet, and it had been so long since the child had heard a human voice.

"Wait," the girl repeated.

The child trembled, torn between hunger for companionship and a fear for its life. It hopped from one foot to another, in an agony of indecision.

The girl reached into her basket and took out an apple and small loaf of brown bread wrapped in a cloth. "Are you hungry?" she asked.

The child could smell the bread, and its mouth watered. Still it was suspicious. Was this a trick? There had been tricks before. No one could be trusted, except the hermit.

The girl sank to her knees, making herself less threatening. She waggled a piece of the bread in her outstretched hand. "Take it," she said.

The child took a small step forward, lured as much by the girl's voice as by the perfume of the fresh bread. Its keen nose also registered the scent of the girl herself, a mixture of wood and tallow smoke and baking. The child took another step forward. It could see the girl's pale, clean skin, her blue eyes, and a few strands of blond hair escaping from the rim of her white cap. The girl's hands were pink from the cold, and her knuckles were raw. The child snatched the bread and darted away.

The girl didn't move. She just nodded and smiled reassuringly. "That's it," she said. "Eat. I've got more."

Keeping its eyes fixed on the girl, the child tore into the bread. How hungry it was! The piece disappeared in a minute. Then the child regretted its greed, for right away its stomach began to ache. After so long in the shadow land, perhaps it should have eaten more cautiously.

The girl held out the apple next, and the child took that, too, though it didn't eat it.

"Are you living here?" the girl asked. "My mother sent me out to the shrine, to tidy it up. We're not supposed to, of course. And I don't know what I can do, because they took the statue of the Virgin away and broke it up. But I'll do what I can."

She stood up and walked to the spring beneath the broken arch. The child followed her, hanging back. The girl picked up half a dozen birch twigs from the ground to make a simple brush, and she swept away the fallen leaves from the low wall around the pool and the ledge beneath the arch where the statue used to stand.

Then she turned to the hermit's cell, sweeping out the leaves. She poked around in the empty fireplace, clearing the dust. The child slunk in behind her to watch. The girl talked a lot. She chatted away as she worked, explaining what she was doing. Although she seemed relaxed, the child was aware that the girl was still wary, keeping watch.

Something caught the girl's attention: a loose brick at the back of the fireplace. "Oh!" she said, squatting in front of the hearth. "Oh! Look what I've found."

She tugged at the brick. Her efforts dislodged a fat lump of soot that fell into the hearth, releasing a puff of fine black dust that settled on her face and apron.

"Oh!" she exclaimed again, wiping the soot from her eyes. She pulled out the brick and thrust her hand into the hole behind. She took out a small pewter cup on a piece of broken chain and showed it to the child.

"This is for the spring," she said. "It used to be fastened

in the wall, so people could drink. There's something else though, farther in."

She put the cup on the hearth and again reached into the hole. This time she drew out a large bundle of ancient parchment, haphazardly folded and rolled. The papers cracked as she pulled them open.

The child hopped from one foot to the other, peering over the girl's shoulder. The parchment was moldy and brown-stained, and it smelled unpleasant, except for the faintest familiar aroma of the hermit that clung to it. Still, the black ink marks were clear to see.

The girl glanced at the words. "Latin," she said. "Prayers." She stuffed the parchment back into the fireplace niche and replaced the cup and brick. "It will be safer here," she said. "Papers can be dangerous. We have to be careful."

The child didn't understand what the girl was talking about, but it squatted beside her. They were very close to each other now, and the girl wrinkled her nose. The child realized its own smell must be very strong.

"Where are you from?" the girl asked. "Have you lived here a long time? Are you an orphan?"

The child stared into the girl's small, oval face, studying her features. She had fair lashes and shapely pale pink lips. Her teeth were clean and white. The girl stared back with equal curiosity.

"Can you speak?" she said softly. "Do you understand me?"

The child frowned. Then it nodded. Yes, it understood perfectly. Could it speak? Once—before this last long, long sojourn in the shadow land—yes, it could. The child was beginning to remember. Memories of the ordinary world were coming back. But it had to be patient, not grab, not want it all at once.

It opened its mouth. "Yes," it said. The sound was like a croak, the voice unused for so long. "Yes," it repeated. "I can speak." But the words came out slowly, as though the child had to find each one.

The girl smiled, her eyes shining. "My name is Elizabeth Dyer," she said. "What are you called?"

This was the question the child had dreaded. It wrinkled its face, knowing not to try to force the remembering but to let it happen of its own accord. It closed its eyes. At last a doorway seemed to open in its mind.

The child gave a profound sigh and turned to Elizabeth. "Isabella," it said. "My name is Isabella Leland."

2

Visitors

lizabeth hurried back toward the town of Maumesbury. Already the afternoon was gloomy, the evening swiftly drawing in. Her dress was sooty, and mud clung to the hem of her skirt. Her excitement, however, exceeded her worries about the scolding she might receive when she got home. She had left Isabella at the hermit's cell with the rest of the bread and a warning not to stray from the shrine. Elizabeth wanted to keep this extraordinary discovery to herself. A green girl! How strange she was, moving like an animal. And the way she smelled—of mud and earth mixed with some sweet and strange perfume.

Elizabeth had to think carefully what to do next. If Isabella was found by someone else, she might be taken away before Elizabeth had a chance to work out a plan. She had heard of wild children before, like Romulus and Remus, the twins in ancient Rome, who were raised by wolves. Had Isabella been raised by wolves? But she could talk. So . . . not lost as a baby, then. Perhaps as a child?

Elizabeth trotted through the forest. The trees gave way

to fields. Not far ahead was the crossroads; then the river and the town on the hill. The sun was sinking. Light reflected on long puddles in ruts left by cart wheels. Threads of smoke rose from the houses. The broken ruins of the old abbey were plain to see, rising above the level of the rooftops.

Elizabeth was hungry, having given all her food to the wild girl, but her thoughts were taken up by her marvelous discovery. At first she had been afraid when she'd spied the low shape leaning over the spring. It was dun colored from a distance, with a thick pelt hanging over its back, and she'd thought it was a wolf. Then the creature began to beat its head with its hands, and she feared it was something unholy—a goblin or a lunatic. She was torn between terror and curiosity, but she didn't run. Slowly, she inched her way toward the creature, trying to get a better view, to find out what it was.

The creature threw itself on the ground in a kind of tantrum, and Elizabeth stepped closer. Clumsily she broke a stick beneath her boot. The next moment the two were face to face, and Elizabeth realized she was looking at a human being. A girl.

The wild girl's hair was very long, hanging in heavy brown clumps right to her knees. And her skin was green! Yes, it was truly green—the pale face dappled, the arms and legs mottled the colors of moss and oak. Green patches also covered the backs of the hands, though when Elizabeth offered the bread, she saw that the girl's palms were white. She also saw that the wild girl—Isabella—had long nails on her hands and feet. Like claws.

She guessed Isabella was about the same age as she. It was hard to be sure, because the wild girl wore only a torn brown tunic, and she was very thin. She didn't look frail, though. She looked strong. She would have to be, Elizabeth thought, to survive on her own in the forest.

Elizabeth hurried through the crossroads. The place was haunted. Several years earlier a robber had been hanged and buried there, outside the town, and after dark people avoided it. But Elizabeth was nearly home now. She crossed the bridge over the river and ran up the steep cobbled hill to the marketplace.

She and her family lived in a house on Silver Street, among the other merchants. Theirs was the largest house on the street, with colored glass in the front window. Despite appearances, however, the family was not prosperous. Their loyalty to the Roman Catholic Church had cost them dearly.

Elizabeth's father, Edward Dyer, was often away on business. But he made little money, because no one wanted to work with him. Any coins the family managed to scrimp and save went to educate Elizabeth's older brother, Robert, at the university in Oxford. So they had only one servant now. That meant Elizabeth, her mother, Jane, and her younger sister, Esther, had to take on the work of the household. It wasn't easy for the girls, wearing castoffs when the other merchants' daughters paraded about in new dresses. Elizabeth's hands had grown red and chapped from scrubbing vegetables and helping with the laundry, while the other girls read poetry and learned to play the lute.

Elizabeth opened the front door and took off her muddy boots. Inside, the house was dark, the candles not yet lit.

"Elizabeth? Is that you?" a voice came from another room.

"Yes, Mother," Elizabeth called out, quickly brushing crumbs of dirt from the bottom of her skirt. She put her boots to one side and replaced them with a very old pair of woolen slippers.

"Elizabeth, come here!"

She hurried through the living room to the kitchen at the back of the house, where Mary, the housekeeper, was tending a pot over a fire in the large hearth. After the chill of outdoors, the kitchen was hot and bright. Esther was sitting on a stool by the side of the fire, fussing over a piece of embroidery. Jane was standing beside the long wooden table.

"Where have you been?" she said. "I was afraid for you. I shouldn't have sent you on your own. What was I thinking?"

Elizabeth gazed at her mother. There was a miniature portrait, painted when her mother was just sixteen and newly engaged to be married, that hung on the parlor wall. In this picture Jane was a beautiful young woman with a wide, pale forehead and curls of golden hair. Twenty years later it was hard to find the glowing girl in the grown woman. Jane was thin, and her body sagged. Her face was always gray and tired.

"I'm sorry to be late," Elizabeth said. "But you see? I am safely home."

Mary turned to look at her, still stirring at the pot. Esther put down her embroidery.

"Did you find the saint's shrine? Did you go the way I told you?" Jane asked.

Elizabeth nodded.

"What is it like?"

"Broken. Deserted. I tidied it, as you asked. Swept out the leaves."

"Did you pray?"

Elizabeth nodded, but she looked away from her mother. She hadn't prayed. The wild girl had distracted her. The prayers had been forgotten. Her mother looked at her closely, perhaps sensing the untruth. Elizabeth's cheeks burned.

"Did anyone see you?" Jane asked softly. "It was a foolish undertaking, but I wanted it done. Did anyone see you?"

Still staring at the table, Elizabeth shook her head. This was perhaps only half a lie. Isabella did not count. Isabella didn't belong to the ordinary world. She wasn't a threat to them.

Jane still regarded her carefully. "Well done," she said at last. "Go again, but not too soon. Take your basket, and if anyone asks where you're going, say that you're looking for mushrooms or firewood. People know we haven't the servants to do all the work anymore. And the Virgin Mary, she will see we haven't forgotten her. Saint Jerome will pray for us."

Jane crossed herself, and Mary nodded and crossed herself as well. It was a risky, secretive business, clinging to the old faith.

Elizabeth helped her mother and the housekeeper prepare supper. If her father had been home, they would have lit a fire in the main room. Tonight, though, they would eat in the warmth of the kitchen.

Edward had been away a long time. He had traveled

across Europe to Venice, hoping to make money importing silks and spices. His letters were infrequent, and his family missed him dreadfully. Somehow their straitened circumstances didn't matter so much when they were all together. Edward rallied their pride in their faith, telling them how generations of Dyers had served the great abbey, reminding them of the great secret they cherished—a trust bestowed upon the family by the church long ago, a secret they would protect even unto death.

Elizabeth sighed. Sacred trusts were all very well, but they didn't ward off the cold or help pay the fines the family faced for not attending Protestant church services. When Edward and Robert were away, the ardor of Elizabeth's faith faded. Life fell apart at the seams.

The womenfolk dined on coarse bread and broth made with barley, onions, and root vegetables. Mary lit a tallow candle that cast a dim yellow light on the table, then brought them stewed apples and a handful of raisins. Esther was chatting on and on about her afternoon helping with the baking, but Elizabeth paid little attention. She wriggled on the bench, her mind full of Isabella.

After the meal they sat together in the warm space before the hearth, and Jane told them a story from the Bible. Then they bowed their heads and prayed for a blessing, for the health and safety of their father and brother, for the forgiveness of their sins and the restoration of the true church. When the candle began to die, the girls left the comfort of the kitchen and made their way through the dark, cold house and up the stairs to the bedroom they shared.

Elizabeth lay awake beside her sister for a long time.

They went to bed early now, because candles were expensive, and she couldn't stop thinking about the wild girl. What would she be doing now? Where did she sleep? How cold and dark it must be in the forest, how frightening to be alone. Elizabeth shivered, pulling the blanket closer around her body, sensing the warmth of Esther close beside her. Elizabeth had to find some way of bringing Isabella back to life—to human life, with clothes and a home and a family to be with. She had to rescue her. This would not be easy.

Outside, Elizabeth could hear the voices of men as they walked home from the taverns. The moon rose into the space of the little bedroom window. A dog barked. Esther gave a tiny snore and hiccup in her sleep. The stairs creaked as Jane made her way to bed.

Elizabeth tried to will herself asleep, but she was wound up tight, thinking about what she should do. Tomorrow she would go to the forest again, with food and something for Isabella to wear. Complicated plans unfolded in her head. She tossed and turned, growing hot and itchy.

Finally, she drifted into sleep—and dreamed that the wild girl was eating the sheaf of papers they'd found in the fireplace niche. Elizabeth scolded her for destroying a piece of the old religion, and Isabella was sick, bringing up long shreds of parchment with the words still written upon them, except that the words didn't make sense. Then she began to beat her head again. The sound of the blows was shocking and loud.

Elizabeth jolted awake, her heart thundering. Someone was knocking on the door.

She was afraid. Who was it, coming in the night? The moon had sunk from the window. It was very late. The knock came again, a low, insistent thud.

She climbed out of bed and hurried into her mother's room, the floorboards icy beneath her bare feet. Jane looked very peaceful when she was asleep, as though her worries had fallen away. Elizabeth didn't want to wake her, but the knocking came again. She ran to the window and looked down to the street in front of the house. Two men were standing there, heavily cloaked. One turned a familiar face up to the window.

Elizabeth's heart seemed to jump to her mouth. "Robert!" she said aloud. Then, "Mum, wake up. Wake up. Robert's here!"

Jane's eyes flicked open. "Robert?" she said. "What's happened to him?"

"He's here! Outside the door!"

Not waiting for Jane to climb out of bed, Elizabeth ran out of the room and down the stairs. She drew back the bolt on the front door. Mary was behind her now, having come from the kitchen, where she slept, tugging a shawl over her shoulders. Elizabeth flung open the door.

The two men stepped over the threshold. They were well wrapped against the weather. Robert's companion was swathed around the neck and face with a woolen scarf.

"Robert!" Elizabeth cried, flinging herself into her brother's arms, not minding the icy cold of his coat against her warm body. He laughed, ruffling her hair with his hand.

Jane came down the stairs, a blanket over her long white shift. She stretched out her arms for Robert. "Quick, Mary, light a candle and revive the fire," she said. "I want to see my son!"

Mary nodded and hurried into the kitchen. Little Esther emerged from the girls' bedroom, very sleepy, and trailed after the others. Robert and his guest were given chairs close to the kitchen fire while Mary warmed food for them. Jane perched upon a stool beside Robert. Her pale blond hair was loose over her shoulders, her face bright and happy. Elizabeth stood to one side, hopping from one cold foot to another, as the men slowly warmed and took off their hats and coats and scarves.

How grown-up Robert looked—and how handsome, she thought. Hardly like the brother she remembered. At nineteen he was a man, with a man's voice and a man's confidence. He was not as blond as she and her mother and sister. His eyebrows were dark, his hair wood-colored and trimmed to his shoulders, and he had a neat beard.

Elizabeth studied their guest. He was older than Robert by some ten years, she guessed, strongly built, with curly black hair and a beard.

While the men dined, the womenfolk waited patiently, near bursting with curiosity about the identity of Robert's companion and the need for a journey by night. But it would be rude and disrespectful to ask. Esther clung tightly to her sister's nightdress, intimidated by the stranger but eager not to miss any of the excitement. Jane stared at Robert, her face so keen and hungry she looked as though she wanted to eat him up. But Elizabeth sensed the change between them: Robert was a man now, his mother an old woman who must wait on him.

"I'm sorry to wake you," Robert said at last. "But I think you will understand the need for discretion and speed. I want to introduce you to a very important friend of mine." He gestured toward the other man. "This is Thomas Montford. He is a priest and a Catholic, and he has come from the seminary at Douai in France. He has a mission—to bring the English, his countrymen, back to the true faith. He has spoken secretly to Catholics at the university and celebrated Mass in private rooms. But the authorities got wind of him and what he was doing, and it was necessary for us to leave as soon as we could."

Jane drew back and put her hand over her mouth.

Thomas spoke. "Thank you for the shelter you've provided me," he said. "I understand your family follows the true faith. Your son has been an ally and a support for me these last months, and when I was in danger, he offered the safety of your home."

Jane didn't look at the priest. She turned to Robert. "Do you know what you bring upon us?" she whispered. "Do you know what would happen if it was found out we harbored this man? For pity's sake! Do we not suffer enough for our faith already? What about your sisters, Robert? What about your own safety? Do you understand what the authorities would do to you?"

Robert stared at his mother, and his lip trembled. For a moment he looked like the boy Elizabeth remembered. He was about to speak when the priest put up his hand.

"Do you think I don't know the peril I bring with me?" Thomas asked. His voice was rich and warm, and his eyes, fixed on Jane, were passionate. "I have celebrated Mass in people's homes, and I have spoken out about the need for England to return to the Catholic faith and denounce the heretic queen. If I am caught, I will be tried and convicted of treason. Do you think I don't understand the penalty? I would be tormented to reveal the names of my fellows, and then I would be executed."

Jane's breathing was fast and shallow. She couldn't draw her eyes from the priest's face. Elizabeth stared, too. Her mouth was dry. She couldn't swallow.

Thomas spoke more gently now. "If the people of England aren't taken back to Rome, they will not find salvation," he said. "They will be doomed to an eternity of torment in hell. Our Lord Jesus Christ was beaten and executed for his faith, and I am prepared to take the same risk to follow in his footsteps. All I ask is that you hide me here for a time, until the furor in Oxford has passed and I can move on again. There are more Catholic sympathizers in the north, and that is where I will go."

"We must help him," Robert said.

Jane nodded. She wiped her nose on the sleeve of her shift and crossed herself. "You're right. We must," she said. She turned to Thomas. "Forgive me my doubt and fear. We will do whatever we can. Will you pray for us?"

"Of course," said the priest.

They all fell to their knees, and he spoke a Latin blessing over their heads.

3

Thomas Montford

lizabeth got up early the next morning and hurried to the kitchen to help her mother and Mary prepare breakfast for Robert and the priest. The small store of food was exhausted in honor of the guests, and the women hovered around them, anxious to give them a good meal.

As the men ate pork chops, nuts, cheese, and apples, Robert told his mother and sisters about life at Oxford—the long lessons in Greek and Latin and mathematics, his cold lodgings, and the miserable landlady who grumbled about the hours he kept. He moaned about the poor clothes he wore, compared with the bright silks and furs adorning the richer students, though Elizabeth noted his clothes were still finer and warmer than her own. She loved her brother, but listening to him, she wondered if he truly understood how hard it was for his mother and sisters to live on the meager sum left over after paying for his education. His student poverty seemed an adventure—not the day-after-day grind endured at home, the endless cutting back, the poor food and hard work.

Elizabeth sighed, but it was hard to be cross with Robert for long. He looked so happy to be home, and their mother had come alive again in his presence. Now he was leaving, heading back to Oxford and entrusting Thomas Montford to their care. He would walk to the crossroads and take the coach on the long, muddy journey to the university.

After the meal Robert led the way to the front door. He and the priest shook hands and embraced awkwardly. Then Robert threw his arms around his mother and kissed her, hard, on the cheek. "Goodbye," he said, reluctantly letting her go. "Take care of Thomas and yourselves."

He turned to his sisters, embraced Esther, and patted Elizabeth on the head. "Be good," he said.

They all stood together a moment, the mother and her three children, Mary, and the priest. Elizabeth squeezed her eyes shut, wanting the interlude to last. *Please, God; please, Holy Mother; please take care of us,* she prayed silently, longing for safety, for her family to be together again soon.

"I have to go," Robert said, breaking the spell. His face was tired and white, and his eyes watered. For a moment Elizabeth thought he was about to weep, but he coughed loudly and turned away. Then he straightened up, becoming a man again. He opened the front door and stepped out into the bitterly cold air. Beyond his head, the sky was washed out—a pale dawn with a powdering of red over the rooftops. One last star twinkled as he picked his way along the cobbled street. He looked back and waved awkwardly; then he disappeared down the hill.

Mary and Esther left the cold doorway, and the priest returned to the kitchen. But Jane didn't move. Finally,

Elizabeth tugged on her mother's sleeve. "Come in, it's cold," she said. "He's gone now."

Jane pressed her lips together. Her body was stiff and resistant, like a piece of wood.

"Mum, please."

Jane shivered. "I'm sorry," she said, wiping her nose on the back of her hand. "Elizabeth, I'm so afraid. I have a terrible feeling." She pressed her fingers to her chest, above her heart. "I don't know why, but I can't help it."

"What? What is it?"

Jane stared over Elizabeth's head. "It will kill me," she said. "It will be more than I can bear. I've tried so hard. I've endured so much. But this—this will be the end of me."

"What?" Elizabeth cried again. "What's going to happen?"

"I'm so afraid for him," Jane said. "He's so young and brave. But I have a premonition. I don't think he will ever come home. I don't think I will ever see him again."

Elizabeth swallowed hard. "You don't know that," she said. "How can you say so?"

But Jane wasn't listening. Tears leaked from her eyes.

"You don't know that," Elizabeth repeated. "You mustn't say it. And *we* are still here, Esther and I, and Father will be home soon."

Jane nodded, holding her daughter briefly against her. But her eyes were still on the street.

Elizabeth went to the kitchen to eat her own meager breakfast. Thomas was sitting on a stool by the fire, staring at the flames as if lost in thought. He didn't seem to notice her as she ate and observed him. His cheeks were ruddy from the fire, his lips still moist from his breakfast. Nothing about his appearance suggested priestliness. He wasn't lean from fasting or pale from hours in prayer. Instead, he looked like a man who could wrestle and ride to hounds, who would spend his days in the sun and weather and his evenings relishing hearty meals.

Is he afraid? Elizabeth wondered. *What is he planning?* She had heard stories about priests who had been captured and charged with treason, each suffering terrible torments and a bloody execution. Now Thomas Montford had brought those dangers to her home, and the threat had spread out to cover them all.

The priest sat up straight and turned to Elizabeth. "Your brother has told me a great deal about your family," he said. "He told me you were clever and lively and never stopped talking. But you are quiet this morning. Are you afraid, Elizabeth?"

Elizabeth put down her crust. She tried to swallow the half-chewed ball of bread in her mouth, but it seemed to lodge in her throat like paper. "Yes," she finally managed to say. "Yes, I am afraid." The priest intimidated her, but she lifted her face and looked directly at him. His eyes were green, and lines curved from the corners in a way that suggested he was a man who often laughed. He smiled now, and his face looked so warm and generous that Elizabeth's shyness melted away. She smiled back.

"Aren't *you* afraid?" she asked.

"Of course," he replied. "But what I have to do is so important, I put my fears to one side. I see them and I say how-do-you-do to them, and then I ignore them. Do you understand? My fears are still there, but I don't let them worry and gnaw at me. The job has to be done, Elizabeth. I heard God's voice, and he wasn't to be put off."

Elizabeth's eyes widened. "God spoke to you?"

The priest nodded. "He speaks to all of us, if only we listen."

Elizabeth thought for a moment. Had God ever spoken to her? She prayed every morning and night, counting off the prayers on the clay beads of her precious rosary, the blue paint worn away by her fingers. But no, God had not spoken to her yet, and perhaps she was glad he had not, if he was going to ask her to risk her life as the priest was risking his. Of course, she should be prepared to die for the Lord, as he had died on the cross for her. But Jesus hadn't wanted to die, either. Even *he* had been afraid, had prayed before his crucifixion and asked for the cup of death to pass from him.

Elizabeth's heart was already in turmoil. She missed her father. She'd seen Robert only to lose him again. Now, as she talked to the priest, who risked death every day he remained in England, her eyes filled with tears.

Thomas smiled gently. "God is with us. Take heart," he said. "You have a job, too, you know. Take care of your mother, Elizabeth. Help her and be kind to your sister. Say your prayers. Wait for God to speak to you."

Jane stepped into the kitchen, her face pale from crying. On her hip she carried Esther, whose face was pressed against her mother's neck.

"Don't forget, you have to go to Spirit Hill today," Jane said to Elizabeth.

Elizabeth was dismayed. She'd been planning to go to the

forest to see the green girl again. She had forgotten all about her visit to the manor. "Today?" she said. "I can't go today."

"You *have* to go, Elizabeth. They'll be expecting you," Jane said, looking to the priest for his support.

"Where does she have to go?" he asked.

"To the manor at Spirit Hill. Lady Catherine, the wife of Lord Melibourne, has taken an interest in her. A surprising interest, considering our different faiths."

Thomas frowned. "Very surprising." He turned to Elizabeth. "You serve the lady? You wait on her?"

Elizabeth nodded. Usually her visits to the manor were a treat, a chance to escape the less-than-charming conditions at home. Sometimes Elizabeth read to Lady Catherine, or wrote letters for her, or helped her with her painting. Lady Catherine had also given Elizabeth lessons in Greek and Latin after the money had run out for a tutor at home. But more often, the lady simply wanted someone to talk to. And Elizabeth was paid for her trouble, an important consideration when the family was so short of money.

"Does she talk to you about your faith? Is she spying on the family? Trying to convert you?" the priest asked.

Elizabeth shook her head.

"The lady is proud and unconventional," Jane said. Then she added disapprovingly, "She is a painter. And she is childless."

The priest looked from mother to daughter. Elizabeth realized that he sensed her reluctance to go and wrongly concluded it arose from his presence, because he said, "You must go. Don't worry about me. Behave as though everything were normal, and you'll be fine."

Elizabeth thought of Isabella alone in the forest and bit her lip. She had promised the wild girl she would return. What if Isabella went away or was found by someone else? She imagined the girl waiting—all alone in the cold—for her to return. How long before she gave up and left the shrine, feeling betrayed by her new friend?

Elizabeth sighed. There was nothing she could do.

The manor was a four-mile walk from Maumesbury, and when the weather was bad, it took Elizabeth the better part of two hours. Today the sun was bright, but pale mud from three days of rain stewed the roads, and the journey seemed particularly long and arduous, with the double layer of unease twisting and twitching in her mind. She kept thinking of Isabella, waiting in the forest with nothing to eat. And when she wasn't thinking of Isabella, she thought of the priest hiding in the house and what would happen if anyone found out.

Elizabeth followed the road for two miles before turning off through fields and meadows to the gentle rise of Spirit Hill. She passed through a gateway with stone columns, and at last the manor house rose ahead of her.

Lord Cecil and Lady Catherine Melibourne were very prosperous. Their house was new, and the carefully arranged gardens were laid out with mazes of low shrubs and with archways that, in the summer months, were covered with roses. The manor was a world unto itself, with a dairy, a granary, and a bake house—and a horde of dairymaids, farm laborers, and servants.

Elizabeth walked to the back of the house and pushed

open the door into the kitchen. The room was crowded, and she felt shy making her way through. She was well aware that the servants were suspicious of her because of her Catholic faith. They were all civil enough, because Lady Catherine expected it, but none had offered Elizabeth any kind of friendship.

A fire danced in the wide hearth, and half a dozen men stood in front of it, warming their backs. These men were better dressed than laborers and filled the room with their presence. They were Lord Cecil's men, part of his household. They spoke together in loud voices, joking and boasting. Their big boots were caked with mud, and they carelessly soiled the flagged kitchen floor. Three hounds, brindled brown and white and with long noses, stared up at them, mindful of heavy feet on thin tails and paws.

The cook was busy preparing a late breakfast for the men and spied Elizabeth edging around the crowd. She beckoned her to step forward and thrust a tray into her hands. "Take this upstairs to the mistress," she said. "You're late. She's waiting for you."

Elizabeth took the tray and nodded, grateful to escape. Then she hurried along the corridor and up the stairs.

Lady Catherine was seated at the window when Elizabeth opened the door. The sun was shining on one side of her face and on her hands as she drew a needle and thread through a piece of linen. For an instant the sunlight picked out the blood red of her yarn.

Elizabeth gave a quick curtsey and placed the tray on a table beside her mistress. Upon it was a dull pewter dish that nestled three tawny hard-boiled eggs and two thick slices of bread skimmed with golden butter. Beside them, in a blue china bowl, lay half a dozen dark purple plums. Illuminated in the shadowed room, the fat plums, the smooth-shelled eggs, and the rich butter seemed to burn with color.

The lady gave a little smile and set her embroidery aside. Observing that Elizabeth was admiring her breakfast, she passed her hand over the tray, throwing a shadow across the dishes and momentarily dimming the colors.

"Beautiful, aren't they?" she said. "It seems a pity to eat them. Then again, the sun will have passed away from the window in another hour, and by then the eggs and bread will be cold." She picked up one of the eggs and passed it to Elizabeth, who closed her fingers, feeling the weight and heat of it in her cold hand.

"Please eat," the lady said, looking into the girl's face. "You seem exhausted. Did the walk tire you today?"

Elizabeth nodded. Her legs were trembling. She hardly dared speak, her secret pressed so hard. The fugitive priest . . . a heretic hiding in her home . . . surely Lady Catherine would guess. Wouldn't the secret be obvious in her face, in the windows of her eyes? If she opened her mouth, perhaps the words would just tumble out, giving everything away.

"Sit down. Sit down. Eat," Lady Catherine urged.

Elizabeth sank to the wooden stool beside the window seat. She watched as her mistress took up another egg and cracked the shell with her slim, clever fingers.

Lady Catherine was dressed in a dark yellow gown today. It was thick and warm, with a high collar and a froth of starched lace around the neck, and the sleeves and bodice were decorated with intricate embroideries of birds and flowers. Her dark red hair was brushed back from her fore-head and tucked inside a velvet cap. Her skin was fair and fine, unlike the tough, coarsened complexions of the servants and the women who worked outside in summer sun and biting winter wind. But the lady wasn't young. There was a weariness in her face, a disenchantment. After four years of marriage, there were no children, and Lord Cecil had taken her from the court, where she had been celebrated as a painter of portraits, and closed her up in the quiet country manor.

The life of a court painter was not suitable for a married woman and the wife of a lord, Lady Catherine had told Elizabeth with a lightness in her voice that did not marry with the sadness in her eyes. She still painted at home, undertaking commissions for portraits of fine ladies and friends of her husband when they deigned to leave London. But life seemed to have ebbed away from Lady Catherine over the years of her marriage, despite her manor house and fine dresses. Elizabeth had often wondered if this was one of the reasons Lady Catherine had taken her on as a companion: both she and Elizabeth were outsiders.

When the meal was over, Lady Catherine picked up her embroidery again and told Elizabeth to read to her. Elizabeth opened the pages of *The Iliad* and began, transporting them to sun-baked islands studded in a sapphire sea, to a male world of fierce friendships and passionate enmities, of blood and triumph and grief. She read for an hour, and for a time she was so caught up in the tale, she forgot about the priest and her brother and Isabella waiting alone in the woods.

Suddenly, Lady Catherine lifted her head, listening intently.

Elizabeth stopped reading. Then she heard it, too—a clatter of hooves as horses skidded to a halt at the front of the house, and men's voices shouting. The blood seemed to stop in her veins as all her worries rushed back. She dropped the book. "What—what—" she stammered.

Lady Catherine stared at her. "It's only horses," she said. "Someone has arrived."

She and Elizabeth hurried to a window at the front of the house. They looked down on two men on horseback, their steeds pawing the ground with muddy legs, necks slicked with sweat.

The men of the household stepped out to meet the visitors, an unspoken communication taking place between them. Elizabeth could see it, the sizing up—Lord Cecil's men eyeing the visitors, sauntering about, displaying how numerous they were, how strong.

The first of the newcomers, a man on a tall gray horse, announced that he had come from court on the queen's business, that his name was Christopher Merrivale. The other man, presumably a servant, waited silently behind his master. Everyone hesitated for a moment, no one moving except for the gray horse, tossing its head and sidling. Then the chamberlain stepped forward and nodded, extending his hand in greeting.

Christopher Merrivale dismounted, handed the reins to his servant, and walked to the house. Just before he crossed the threshold, he looked up to the window where Elizabeth and Lady Catherine stood. His feathered hat tipped back, revealing an oval face framed by long black hair, a single pearl earring glinting. He spotted the watchers and smiled.

Lady Catherine drew a breath, fluttering beside Elizabeth. "Oh, what a fine-looking man!" she said. "Why do you suppose he has come?"

Elizabeth pressed her teeth together, and her lips trembled. Her whole body felt cold. Christopher Merrivale had looked directly at her, and she was certain he could see who she was and what she had to hide.

4

Remembering

he wild girl curled up in the corner of the hermit's cell to sleep. Her stomach growled and churned and her belly hurt, as though the food Elizabeth had given her had tied itself into a hard knot. It was a cold night, but Isabella was used to the cold. She had endured many winters in the hollow tree, lying beneath a blanket of snow. Now she pressed herself against the walls of the cell and wrapped her rug of hair around her as best she could. It rained in the night, and she listened to the drops patter on the lumpish thatch of the roof. Leaks let cold water through, and it lay in puddles on the floor. Isabella had no desire to sleep. Her mind didn't want to let go of the memories of the day: climbing out of the tree, meeting Elizabeth at the fountain, remembering her own name, remembering who she was.

Isabella Leland. She was called something else in the other place, the shadow land of the crow people. Now she repeated her real name over and over. There was still so much to remember of her earthly life. She held on tightly to the fragments she already had.

Isabella Leland.

Would Elizabeth return? Isabella hoped and hoped that she would. Elizabeth had warned her to stay close to the hermit's cell, and Isabella had no intention of leaving if her new friend was coming back to see her again.

The night was very long. The forest was mostly quiet except for the low moan of the wind. Once, she heard the rustle of paws outside the leaky hovel and smelled the sharp, rank scent of a fox. And near dawn, far away, the long, sad call of a solitary wolf wound among the trees. Isabella rose and stepped outside. She drew a deep breath, filling her lungs, her body, with the forest air.

She was glad to be back, despite the cold and the danger. She had stayed with the crow people a long, long time, and her brother, John, was with them still. Isabella missed him. She missed him very much. He was her only family, even if he didn't remember her very well anymore.

Could she find him again and bring him home?

She watched the sun rise, sensing the response of the trees as they stretched their branches to the warmth and light. She felt the threads of energy flow from the tips of their highest leaves down to the tendrils of their deepest roots in the moist, black earth.

She ate Elizabeth's apple. Afterward she drank from the spring and washed her face and hands. The cold water stung, and though she rubbed her arms with a wet wad of scratchy moss, the green did not come off. Her face, she saw in the reflection, was still a dappled leafy color. How strange she looked.

Isabella spent the morning reacquainting herself with

the area around the shrine. She didn't stray far, because she didn't want to miss Elizabeth, but moving stretched out the kinks in her joints and muscles so she could stand upright. It made her warm and brought color to her cheeks. She was glad to be awake again, to be alive.

The day passed quickly enough, but Isabella was always looking out for Elizabeth, and as the light began to fade in the late afternoon, her happiness seeped away. She knew it was too dark now for the girl to find her, and she was deeply disappointed. Why hadn't Elizabeth come? Would she ever come back? Had she changed her mind?

Isabella retreated to the hermit's cell and sat huddled against the wall. She felt empty inside and utterly alone. Now that Elizabeth had abandoned her, she knew no one in this strange new world. She couldn't tell how long she had been asleep, but judging by the changes in the forest and the dereliction of the hermit's cell, many, many years had passed. Jerome and anyone else she might have known from her last visit would be long dead.

When the moon rose, Isabella went to the spring. The wind had died. A slice of moon was reflected on the surface of the water. How still it was, how eerie. Fragile feathers of ice formed over the stones and painted the fallen leaves white. Isabella crouched low, shivering, wrapping her arms about herself to keep warm. She was lost and adrift. She remembered with longing her mother, Ruth, who had died, and her brother, John, who was far away in the other land with the crow people. Both were out of reach.

Isabella closed her eyes, trying to conjure up memories of her life with her mother and baby brother. Her time with the crow people lay between then and now like a dark, form-less mass, a great chasm her mind had to leap to reach the or-dinary days of her first home, her real and only home. A hundred years with the crow people might pass like a single night. Or it might take a dozen days for the Faerie Queen to raise a golden cup from the table to her dark red mouth. How long had Isabella spent in the shadow land? Two hun-dred years? Three hundred? What year was it now?

It was a sweltering summer day in the year 1240 when Isabella saw one of the crow people for the first time. Ruth had tucked baby John into a shawl and tied him onto her back so that she and Isabella could work in the vegetable gar-den, weeding between rows of beans and cabbages. Their tiny cottage, a single room under a messy thatch, was built on the fringes of the forest. But from the garden Isabella could see, in the distance, the town on the hill with its busy abbey. So she saw the man urging on his galloping horse long before he arrived. The horse kicked up a white dust from the dry road. The drumming of hooves, almost impossible to hear at first, grew louder and louder as the rider approached. Then all of a sudden, the horse was upon them, skidding to a halt, laboring for breath.

"Mistress Leland!" the man called.

Slowly Ruth stood up straight. She mopped the sweat from her face.

"It's Mistress Watts . . . she's having the baby. They need you," the rider said. His horse, still excited from the long ride, danced its flinty hooves on the road.

Ruth nodded. She was a small, slight woman with dark

brown hair that twisted into long, slippery curls. Even when she plaited it and tucked the shiny plait under her woolen cap, strands escaped and framed her narrow face, with its pointed chin and dark brown eyes. She smiled now, and turned to the cottage.

"Hurry! She's in a terrible way," the man said, his voice unsteady and his face pink with anxiety. His horse pirouetted, eager to be off again. But Ruth unhurriedly entered the house to collect her things, leaving her daughter to stare at the rider.

Isabella was small for her age, and the horse looked impossibly tall. She noticed how the man gave quick little glances at the cottage, curious and nervous at the same time. Like others, he seemed afraid to come too close.

It was a strange place, Isabella knew. Shadows seemed to fall in the wrong spots. From time to time—without any discernible breeze—the bundles of dried herbs hanging from the beams would begin to nod. A wooden bowl placed on the table at night might be found, the next morning, upon the doorstep. But it was her home.

"Please hurry," the man said again as Ruth emerged from the cottage with a leather bag. "You'll ride with me."

Ruth nodded. She lifted John from her back, kissed his forehead tenderly, and handed him to Isabella. "Follow me on foot," she said, tying the shawl around her daughter's shoulders to make a sling for the baby. "You know the place?"

Isabella nodded.

Ruth stepped up to the horse and its dangerous dancing feet, but the animal settled when she drew near, reaching out its frothy nose to snuff at her. The man leaned over and easily pulled her up behind him. He clapped his heels against the horse's sides, and they were off, flying up the road toward town.

Within minutes a huge, hot hush fell over the house and garden again. Only a few motes of dust still spun in the air where the horse had been.

Isabella sighed and wiped her face on the back of her hand. Carrying the baby, she would need half an hour to reach town, and the sun was relentless. She adjusted the shawl to cover John's head and began the journey.

The town reared before her, the houses sheltering in the shadow of the huge abbey—home to hundreds of monks and a center of learning renowned across Europe. Maumesbury Abbey owned much of the town, a vast library, granaries, trout ponds, vineyards on the flanks of the hill—even a leper hospital on the edge of town.

As the rider had said, Mistress Watts was in a terrible way. The whole neighborhood seemed beaten into silence by the heat and by the sound of the laboring woman's screams, which could be heard streets away. Even the dogs cowered and whimpered in the shadows. Isabella stopped by the house in Silver Street. The upstairs window was open, to provide some fresh air for the poor woman, but this only served to make her sufferings more public. John shifted, as though the sounds of distress from the bedroom had woken him. Isabella went to the back of the house and knocked on the kitchen door. The old woman who answered scowled at her.

"What do you want?" she said. Then she seemed to guess who Isabella was, because her expression changed to one of grudging respect. "You're the midwife's girl," she said. "Go on upstairs."

Isabella stepped past, noticing from the corner of her eye how the servant stared at baby John and made a gesture, perhaps the sign of the cross.

The bedroom was busy with women, all fussing around the central actor in the drama—Mistress Watts, who struggled and bellowed on the high bed. She was a big woman, with huge white thighs and a belly like a mountain. Beside her, small and neat, was Ruth, the only element of serenity in the room. Mistress Watts held on to Ruth's arm with both hands, squeezing hard. Isabella had seen it many times before, in low hovels, in grand houses, even once at the side of a road: women, wretched with exhaustion and pain, gripping her mother as she encouraged and reassured them, giving them a beacon of hope and comfort. Isabella was sure Ruth's skin must be bruised, but she knew her mother would not complain.

After some time, there was a moment of calm in the labor. Mistress Watt stared into Ruth's face, as if placing all her hope of delivery on the slight shoulders of the midwife. Then she was convulsed by a great wave of pain, and the baby was born all at once, pink and red and slippery, the cord glittering like a string of jewels.

In an instant the mood of the gathered women turned. There was a cry of delight. "It's a boy, Mistress. A lovely boy!" And they all came close, relatives and servants alike, to peer at the baby and marvel at him, to pat and congratulate the new mother, who smiled as she panted, her eyes bright with happiness.

With quick, deft movements Ruth cut the cord, cleaned the baby, wrapped him in a soft cloth, and handed him to his mother. Mistress Watts, her thick hair tumbled over her shoulders, gave the midwife a deep look, full of gratitude.

Mistress Watts looked beautiful, Isabella thought. The struggling animal she had been just minutes earlier was transformed into something magical, almost luminous, like the picture of the Virgin Mary in the church window when the sun shone through.

Isabella helped prepare a tea made of dried raspberry leaves to aid Mistress Watts's recovery. She felt proud of her mother, who was so generous and modest. Already Ruth was packing up her things, so that the family might celebrate together.

One of the servants tapped Isabella on the shoulder. "Go to the kitchen," she said. "The woman will give you something to drink."

Isabella glanced at her mother, who nodded and said, "I can manage." But Isabella hesitated. The tone of Ruth's voice troubled her. Was something wrong?

"Go on," her mother urged.

Isabella was reluctant to return to the dour woman in the kitchen, but she was too shy to protest before so many strangers. Slowly she made her way down the stairs. John weighed very heavily upon her now. She was tired.

"They said you'd give me a drink," she whispered to the kitchen woman.

The woman frowned. "Sit down," she said. Isabella untied the shawl and sat with baby John on her lap. He waved his arms up and down and grinned at the old woman, who smiled back, despite herself.

Bent over, shuffling, the old woman drew a mug of small beer from a barrel and handed it to Isabella, who took a quick sip. The drink was cool and earthy, and she savored the taste, moving the beer around in her mouth.

News of the safe delivery had reached the kitchen, because the old woman said: "Your mother will be well rewarded. This child has been a long time coming. The mistress has always miscarried before."

Isabella drank again, not knowing how to answer, wishing the woman wouldn't stare at her so hard.

"They tell me your father died," the old woman said. "Your mother couldn't heal him then."

"It wasn't her fault," Isabella shot back, unable to hear Ruth criticized unfairly. Her father, John Leland, had died when she was very young, after a battle in which he was compelled to fight for the Lord Marchers, powerful nobles who guarded the frontier between England and Wales. He hadn't died fighting, Ruth had told her. He was wounded and had contracted an infection on the journey home. A pointless death that Ruth could have prevented if she'd been at hand. When she spoke of her husband and the manner of his death, Ruth's eyes darkened. It was the only subject likely to put her out of humor.

"Beg pardon." The woman's voice was cold, and she still stared, making Isabella shy again. She gazed into her cup, hoping to escape the woman's scrutiny.

"So who's the baby's father?" the woman persisted.

It occurred to Isabella that this was the question the old

woman had wanted to ask all along. And it was one she could not answer. She continued to stare into the wooden mug and simply shrugged. Only Ruth knew who baby John's father was. It was something she would not discuss with her daughter.

Sometimes Isabella speculated on who it might be, among the men of the town and outlying villages, but she had no real idea. Single women were vulnerable, and she suspected someone might have taken advantage of her mother. Once, she'd overheard someone suggesting John's father was a devil from the woods, and she had repeated these evil tidings to her mother. But Ruth had dismissed the suggestion with a laugh. For all intents and purposes, the pregnancy had come from nowhere.

At last Ruth came downstairs, her face pale and damp from the heat. She picked up her baby and took Isabella's hand, and they left the house in Silver Street. They were no longer needed there.

5

Faerie

sabella brightened as she and her mother walked away from the town. They talked as they went, John high on his mother's back and soon fast asleep, the side of his face pressed against her shoulder. Ruth began to smile again, too, and her words were cheerful. Isabella glanced at her mother. Ruth was always laughing, always in good spirits—even when she was treating patients with terrible afflictions, setting broken bones, or cleansing infected wounds. Perhaps this was part of her success, thought Isabella. Her good humor and happiness were contagious.

Isabella had already attended the delivery of babies with her mother and had assisted her when laborers or soldiers needed muscle and skin stitching. One day this job would be hers, and although the prospect did not upset her, she wondered if she could ever be as strong and generous as her mother. It was hard to imagine. Despite the heat, Isabella gave a little shiver, and tension gripped the pit of her stomach.

Ruth glanced at her. "What's the matter?" she asked.

Isabella shook her head. "Nothing. I was just—just thinking about how clever you are. I'll never be as good as you."

Ruth smiled. "Yes, you will," she said. "You know so much already."

"It's not the knowing I'm talking about, it's how you are," Isabella said. "You help people just by being with them." Ruth's face clouded, and Isabella felt again the unease she had sensed in her mother before. "What are you thinking about?" she asked. "What's wrong?"

Now Ruth sighed. "It's the baby," she said, looking at the road and not at her daughter. "The new baby. When I placed my hand on his chest"—she cupped her fingers in the air to demonstrate—"there was something wrong with his heart, Isabella. I didn't tell them. I couldn't bear to. They've waited so long for this child, and she was so happy. But the rhythm of his heart was all wrong."

Isabella looked at her mother's face. Plenty of babies died before they were a year old. Illness picked them off, the flux, measles, bouts of fever. But this baby was more important than most. This was an only child, a son to carry the family name, and the Wattses were powerful people.

That vague sense of unease haunted them the rest of the day. Then, in the long midsummer twilight, Ruth put John on her back, and she and Isabella left their little cottage and entered the forest. Under the cover of young leaves, the footpaths were emerald tunnels. Ribbons of perfume trailed from honeysuckle vines that clasped tree branches. Flat pink dog roses bloomed on tough, thorny stems.

As they walked, Ruth told Isabella about the properties

of herbs and plants, pointing out examples—which leaves might be eaten as a salad, what bark could be brewed as a tea to treat the pains of toothache, which roots might be dug up, dried, and ground to provide a cure for stomach cramps. These lessons had been often repeated, so that Isabella could remember them. Ruth's mother had also been a healer, and hers before that. So Ruth had inherited a wealth of herbal and medical lore from generations of wise women. Everyone came to her for help. Even monks from the abbey, many of whom were accomplished doctors and surgeons, sought her out.

Isabella absorbed the beauty of the forest, decked in golden green. Her mother stopped talking as the sun slowly set. Leaves gently stirred in the treetops and then became still. Everything was silent. There wasn't a note from a bird or a chatter from a squirrel in the branches. It was as if the forest held its breath.

Ruth followed their little path to a brake of holly and elder trees, which gave way to a clearing where bright, cold water bubbled into a shallow pool. An old willow tree stretched its branches over the water. Dozens of ribbons and strips of colored cloth had been tied to the willow. In the still air they hung limp, some stained with age and weather, some glossy and new. It was a part of the old religion, this offering to the tree and the spring. Women from the town and the surrounding villages often made wishes and tied up their ribbons, though the priest had forbidden it. Sometimes they tried to ease their consciences, claiming the shrine was dedicated to the Virgin Mary. But Ruth had told Isabella that the spring had received offerings long before the Christian religion came to England.

Ruth took John from her back and handed him to Isabella. She looked very serious. "Do you see that rowan to the west?" she said, pointing out a slender tree. "I want you to take John and wait with him over there, in its shadow. Whatever you see, whatever happens, you must stay there, and you must be especially careful that your brother stays within the shadow of the tree. Do you understand?"

Isabella nodded. She knew this was where her mother came to be with the crow people, the faeries who lived in the wood. For as long as she could remember, her mother had told her stories about the Queen of the Faeries and her royal court. Perhaps Isabella had dreamed of them, too, before she could walk or talk. Never, though, had she seen them. Sometimes at night her mother went to the forest—occasionally with other women from the village, more often alone—to return with a curious perfume on her cold skin, her hair tangled with twigs and leaves. But she had never allowed Isabella to accompany her before. What had changed her mind? Was it something to do with the new baby and its faulty heart?

Isabella took John and sat beneath the rowan tree. She watched as her mother washed her hands and face in the cold water of the spring. Isabella was excited—and frightened, too. She had longed to see the crow people for so many years. But she knew they were powerful and sometimes cruel. The rowan tree offered protection, because the faeries didn't like it. Hiding in its shadow, she and John would be safe.

Isabella's family had a long connection with the faeries. Mother to daughter, through hundreds of years, they had passed on the colorful history of the faerie people, a treasury of marvelous tales. Before Christian times Isabella's great-grandmothers had been priestesses, links between mortals and the crow people, held in high esteem. Of course, it was different now. People came to Ruth for help when they were ill, but they also treated her with suspicion. She wasn't part of acceptable society.

A curious ripple passed through the forest, and Isabella sat up straighter. Nothing had changed—except there was a charge in the atmosphere, like the moment before a bolt of lightning strikes. She remembered what her mother had told her. Across the ordinary world lay a web of silvery connections, holding stone and seed, bone and fur, ice and wood in a pattern. Behind the web, beyond the pattern, was the shadow land where the crow people lived. They could pass through spaces in the web to the earthly side. Sometimes mortals passed to the shadow land, but they rarely came back, and if they did, a hundred years might have gone by in their absence.

For the very first time, Isabella was aware of the web her mother had described. She could see it in the glint of a stone, the coils of a bramble, the veins of a leaf. The forest seemed to fill her mind, more real than before. It crowded inside of her, too much to hold all at once. At the same time, she sensed how the entire scene could be pulled aside, like a curtain.

What lay beyond?

Ruth stood straight, her long hair loose and blowing in a wind Isabella couldn't feel. Her mother raised her hand, and an arched doorway appeared in the forest.

Lying on the ground beside Isabella, baby John became

agitated, waving his arms and legs in the air, but he didn't cry. "Don't worry," she whispered, stroking his soft cheek. "We're safe here." She stared, trying to see beyond the doorway, sensing in the air the potent and alien perfume of the land of the crow people: cold stone and dust and roses. She was afraid for her mother, yet thrilled by Ruth's power as she stood by the black mouth of the door.

Then the faerie appeared, stepping through the archway.

It was very tall and slender, with long white hands and feet. Isabella somehow knew it was a male, despite the extraordinary beauty of its face and the dark red color of its mouth. Glossy black feathers poured over the faerie's shoulders and covered the long wings folded on his back. Long silky black hair hung down to his thighs. He wore a soft leather cloth around his waist and a large quantity of gold jewelry that glinted dully—a necklace of engraved coins, thick bracelets, a host of rings, a plaited belt.

The shape of the faerie wasn't consistent. From time to time it changed momentarily, a beak pressing out from the face, the long white feet becoming wicked claws. The creature turned his head, perhaps sensing Isabella's presence. Yellow eyes sought her out . . . found her, held her.

Isabella froze. She felt the faerie look into her mind and sift through her trove of memories, the ten short years of her life. The faerie seemed to taste them and spit them out again. It was over in an instant. The faerie looked away, forgetting her, and Isabella was overwhelmed by a sense of her own smallness and unimportance. She was nothing—less than nothing. Her life was insignificant to him, as the life of an ant might be to her.

Ruth still stood before the faerie, unafraid, proud, confident of her own worth and power. The faerie stretched out his hand and placed it on her head in a gesture of blessing. Did they speak to each other? Isabella could not tell. But some kind of communication seemed to pass between the crow man and the mortal woman. She saw Ruth shake her head and gesture to her children sheltering beneath the rowan tree.

Isabella felt so empty and dreary now that the faerie had turned away from her. As heavy as a clod of clay. She wanted to get close to the beautiful creature, so she could cover up her own sense of smallness by worshiping him. She ached to be close to him, to bathe in his majesty, to fall on her knees before him.

She remembered her mother's words and the promise she had made to stay by the rowan tree with her brother. The words rang clearly in her memory. But she was hollow inside. She wanted . . . she wanted so much.

She rose to her feet, and John gave an agitated squawk. Her fever of longing grew. Yes, she had promised, but the promise meant nothing now. Nothing was important except for the faerie. She stepped forward, one foot moving from the shadow of the rowan tree.

A blast of moonlight hit her face. It was a shock, like a splash of cold water. She hadn't noticed nightfall or moonrise in the glow of faerie light around the holy spring.

Isabella hesitated, and baby John grabbed the edge of her skirt with his tiny hand. When she tried to step forward again, he tugged and gave out a squeal. Furious, Isabella whipped round to pull free, but John held on tightly. She wanted to push him away, kick him, hurt him—anything to make him let go. But John looked into her eyes, and his mouth curved into a toothless smile.

Isabella softened. She gazed at his smooth, chubby face, his perfect new skin. The love she felt for him poured over her, and the spell fell away. Now she felt ashamed of her anger. She remembered with horror how just a moment before she'd wanted to kick him and throw him away to be close to the faerie. She scooped him up in her arms, pressed him against her chest, and burst into tears.

Isabella woke, still sitting by the same spring where her mother had called up the crow man so many years before and where, in his turn, Jerome had lived and prayed. For a moment, past and present were confused. Then she remembered where she was.

Isabella had left the shadow land several times before, to visit the ordinary world. But this visit felt different. She didn't want to go back again, except to get John. Then she wanted them both to stay here.

The chilly gray dawn spread over the forest, and Isabella rubbed her cold arms. She waited for Elizabeth.

6

Kit Merrivale

The chamberlain escorted Christopher Merrivale into the long hall, where the household dined. A boy wearing a leather apron hurried after them with a basket of logs to feed the fire. Lady Catherine hesitated outside the room, touching her hair and her face; then she entered. Reluctantly, Elizabeth followed her.

Merrivale doffed his hat and made a sweeping bow. He took Lady Catherine's hand and kissed it. "I am your servant, my lady," he said. "I come here on the queen's business, but I am a friend of Lord Cecil's. He sent his greetings and a letter."

Merrivale unbuckled a pouch on his belt and drew out a sealed and folded page. Lady Catherine took her husband's letter without looking at it and slipped it into her pocket. She invited Merrivale to sit by the fire and ordered the chamberlain to bring beer and food for the visitor and to make sure Merrivale's companion was well cared for. The chamberlain bowed and left the room. Elizabeth hovered in the background, wishing she, too, could slip away, but at least Merrivale paid her no attention.

The long hall, situated at the front of the house, was full of sunlight. It was paneled with wood, and one wall was adorned with a tapestry of knights fighting dragons. Fresh straw and rushes, sprinkled with sprigs of dried rosemary, were spread in a carpet across the floor, and the herbs gave off a tangy perfume underfoot.

Merrivale left a trail of mud across the room. He sat down and signaled to the boy feeding the fire to pull off his filthy boots. Then he stretched his stocking feet to the hearth with a sigh.

Elizabeth frowned. This man had just arrived, and already he was treating the house as his own. And he was young—probably about the same age as her brother. Elizabeth glanced at Lady Catherine, but her mistress didn't seem bothered by Merrivale's manners; she merely drew up a second chair to sit on the other side of the fire.

"May I ask what business it is that brings you here?" she said. "Are you passing through, or will you stay? How is Her Majesty? And life in the court? You know, I was a portrait painter there, before I married."

Elizabeth felt a little embarrassed for her mistress. Lady Catherine was so transparently desperate for news and excitement.

Merrivale held up his hand and laughed, cutting off the stream of questions.

"Lady Catherine's fame lives on at court, even though her husband has buried her in the country," he said smoothly, looking sideways at his hostess to see how she blushed at this piece of easy flattery. Then he went on. "Lord Cecil is hard at work in the queen's treasury, trying to raise money for the navy and battles with the Spanish. I cannot speak of my own business, but I intend to stay here a few days—if you are content to offer me your hospitality."

"Of course," Lady Catherine said quickly. She blushed again and twisted her hands together. "Of course," she repeated, trying to regain her dignity. "We are a loyal and devoted household, and we shall render any service we can to a man who comes on the queen's business."

Merrivale nodded. "I'm grateful," he said.

A serving girl bustled into the room with a tankard and a bowl of hot spiced pork and vegetable broth, and Merrivale ate with good appetite as Lady Catherine looked on.

Elizabeth studied him carefully. She supposed he would be considered handsome, with his fine, pale face, gray eyes, and long dark lashes. He had a narrow mustache and a small pointed beard, and he was well dressed, in a burgundy velvet jacket trimmed with black fur and fastened with a dozen tiny pearl buttons. His stockings had the sheen of silk, and his long boots, drying by the fire, were finely fashioned from soft red leather. His earring shone.

But for all his fine clothes and the effort he obviously lavished on his appearance, Elizabeth didn't like him. There was something about the color of his skin that made her think of the belly of a dead fish. And his eyes were like stones, flat and unresponsive. It was as though he had trained himself to hide his thoughts—a talent that, right now, she wished she possessed.

When he had eaten, Merrivale satisfied Lady Catherine's thirst for court gossip. He told her who was in and out of favor, which of the queen's ladies in waiting had married and to whom. He told her about the theaters and concerts, the entertainments laid on for the foreign ambassadors at the court. Lady Catherine drank it up, asking for details, wanting to hear about the fortunes of the friends she had left behind. Finally, Merrivale shook his head and laughed. He was tired, he said. With her permission, he would speak with his servant and check the horses; then he would rest.

When he left, Lady Catherine was silent for a few moments, still absorbing all the news, still spellbound by her fashionable guest.

Elizabeth glanced out the window. The afternoon light was fading, and she wanted nothing more than to escape the manor and go home.

"Elizabeth," Lady Catherine said, remembering her presence. "Isn't he a wonderful young man? Isn't it exciting to have a visitor?"

"Yes, my lady," Elizabeth replied. "May I go home now? It's getting late, and I don't want to walk in the dark."

Lady Catherine frowned and bit her lip. "I would like you to stay here tonight," she said. "We have a special guest, and I would like you to attend me. I need a lady in waiting. I shall send a message with one of the men to your mother."

Elizabeth paled. "Please," she said. "My mother needs me. I want to go home."

Lady Catherine sat up straight. Her face stiffened. "I'm sure your mother doesn't need you as much as I do, Elizabeth. You will do as I say."

Elizabeth nodded numbly. What choice did she have? The lady did so much for her and was her superior; she was not to be contradicted. Elizabeth thought of her cold, quiet home, her mother and sister sitting by the fire with the priest, who trusted them to hide and guard him. She wanted to be with them, and she needed to do something to help Isabella.

She clenched her teeth, trying to hold back the tears that pricked her eyes, trying to hide her feelings. But she needn't have worried. Lady Catherine wasn't paying attention, her head seemingly full of thoughts about their visitor.

That night Elizabeth shared the cook's bed, a straw mattress in a room off the kitchen. She slept badly, disturbed by the cook's snores and her stink of sweat and spiced meat and by the racing of her own mind. She thought about Isabella and wondered if the wild girl had run away. She thought about Merrivale and convinced herself that he had come in pursuit of the priest, that already he knew where Thomas Montford was hiding. And she ached to be home with her mother, to be lying beside her little sister instead of the cook, who scratched and dribbled in her sleep.

The cook got up before dawn to shout at the girl who laid the fires and to supervise the making of breakfast. Her absence from the bed was a huge relief to Elizabeth. For a while she lay alone and listened to the rain beat against the window. Eventually, the sound lulled her to sleep. But all too soon the commotion in the kitchen—the men calling for their food and cursing at the weather—woke her again.

As the morning wore on, she realized why her mistress had been so eager for her to stay in the house. It would not be proper for Lady Catherine to spend time alone with Master Merrivale, but the constant presence of a lady in waiting made everything respectable.

Merrivale seemed in no particular hurry to get on with whatever important business he had to attend to. He sat by the fire in the long hall with Lady Catherine, and they played cards. Elizabeth sat to one side on a stool, a piece of embroidery in her hands. Merrivale told Lady Catherine to call him Kit. They talked about the court again and discussed people Elizabeth didn't know. It was tedious to attend them. Lady Catherine, whom she liked so much, began to irritate her with bursts of girlish laughter. Merivale frightened her. And worries about her family and thoughts of Isabella went round and round her head.

In the afternoon the rain finally stopped, and they walked outside. The sky was bright and blustery, with rags of clouds and intervals of vivid blue sky, and Lady Catherine showed Merrivale the gardens and grounds. She was proud of her estate, acquainting her guest with the stables, where a dozen satin-coated horses were bedded in deep straw, and the kitchen gardens, where a lad and an old man hacked at the heavy soil among ranks of cabbages and ribby turnip tops. As they walked in the orchards, she recounted how the estate included so many farms and tenants, so many thousands of acres.

"Of course, all of this belonged to the abbey before the Reformation," Merrivale remarked.

When he said this, he didn't look at Elizabeth, who was trailing after them. But she couldn't help thinking that the statement had been dropped into the conversation for her sake. She shivered, pulling her shawl closer around her shoulders.

"Yes," Lady Catherine said. "The abbey was very powerful. Its lands stretched to Cornwall. Of course, it had grown corrupt. Its wealth was used to buy power, and the monks had forsaken their vows and taken wives."

"When it fell, its great library was destroyed," Merrivale said. "That was a dreadful thing. Five hundred years of learning lost."

Lady Catherine nodded. "They say that for years the town was awash with books and manuscripts. People used them to line their boots and light fires and keep the drafts from their homes."

Elizabeth shuddered to think of the scale of destruction. She knew that even now, remnants of the library could be found, slips of illuminated parchment squeezed in the gaps of window frames or lining the thatch of the poorer houses in Maumesbury.

Merrivale and Lady Catherine slowed to a halt at the end of the orchard, and Elizabeth noticed that in the sunlight the lady looked older. The bright light picked out the lines around her eyes, and her lips were pale with cold. Elizabeth also saw that Lady Catherine's hands were shaking.

Lady Catherine touched her face, a nervous gesture. She looked at Merrivale, coloring as she spoke. "What do you know about me, Kit?" she asked. "What do they say at court?"

"Your portrait of the queen is greatly admired," he said with an ingratiating smile. "People still marvel that a woman should be so accomplished and have such powers of expression."

"We were not a wealthy family," Lady Catherine said, her voice trembling. "My father was a painter, and I was his student. That is the reason I took up such unusual employment. And it turned out that I had some natural talent. But I am married now, married to a lord—a remarkable thing for an artisan's daughter." She swallowed and touched her face again, very quickly. Then she went on. "I have no children. At court, they must say I'm barren. They must think my husband's long absences stem from his disenchantment with me."

"No, everyone knows that he is devoted to you," Kit protested.

Elizabeth looked away, embarrassed by the intimacy of the conversation, surprised that Lady Catherine should confide in this stranger. She had not realized how lonely Lady Catherine was, even with a great herd of servants to wait on her and a powerful husband at the court.

Elizabeth was ordered to stay for a second night, and her worries about Isabella dulled. There was nothing she could do now.

The manor was in a state of excitement. To honor their guest, the entire household would dine together at the table in the hall. Musicians were summoned from the town—an elderly man and his son who played the lute and dulcimer. In her husband's absence Lady Catherine sat alone at the head of the table. Elizabeth was to her left; Merrivale was to her right. The Lord's men sat below them; then, farther down, the servants in their varying ranks. They ate well, all of them. Thick slices of bread served as trenchers to soak up the spiced gravy of roasted, sugared meats and stewed vegetables. Afterward they had fruit puddings and cheese. The servants drank small beer, but the lady and her husband's men and Merivale drank pitchers of red wine. She sipped discreetly; the men were less judicious. Their voices grew loud.

Tallow candles burned on the table, filling the room with warm yellow light and a thick, meaty smoke. Elizabeth's eyes watered, and she was drowsy with so much food and the weariness of two nights of broken sleep. She paid little attention to the conversation, until Merrivale began to talk about plots by members of the Roman Catholic seminary in Douai.

"They are sending priests over to England," Merrivale said. "This is nothing to do with matters of faith. These men have one aim: they are heretics who wish to remove Queen Elizabeth from the throne and replace her with a Catholic monarch."

He was addressing Lady Catherine, and the room was thick with noise, but his words were distinct to Elizabeth, as though he had spoken just to her. She stared at the platter before her, the remains of her meal. She forced herself to breathe.

"These men are not just Catholic troublemakers. They are trained to foment revolution," Merrivale went on. He spoke with great seriousness now, and the other men, red in the face from drink, turned from their boasting and jeering to listen—and to whisper one to another.

The scene swam in front of Elizabeth's eyes, as the flickering candlelight alternately hid and revealed eyes . . . noses . . . and mouths moist with wine and words. The men looked like demons, leering and grimacing. Her heart thundered. She felt faint—hot and cold at the same time—and sat back on the long wooden bench, wishing the shadows would swallow her up entirely.

"Is there evidence of this?" Lady Catherine asked.

Merrivale nodded. "Walsingham's spies have uncovered plots, intercepted letters. They've caught a number of the priests."

"And they have confessed?"

"Walsingham is . . . persuasive."

Elizabeth felt sick. Tales of Walsingham, the queen's spymaster and torturer, had spread across the country. She thought of her brother and the man hidden in her house. Had the captured priests told Walsingham about Thomas Montford? Was that why the priest had fled from Oxford to Maumesbury?

The meal Elizabeth had eaten lay like a great weight in her stomach. She picked up her cup, but her hands were shaking, and she couldn't swallow.

The men, drunk and keen to prove their bravery, began to speculate about methods of torture and to describe the spectacle of a heretic's execution they had witnessed on a trip to Tyburn in London, when they had attended their lord at court.

Elizabeth tried to block out the sounds of their voices, the images their words created in her mind. She pressed her nails hard into the palms of her hands, trying to distract herself with pain. Her stomach heaved—surely she would be sick. The room was so hot she could scarcely breathe. All at once the blood seemed to fall from her head. The hall, the men, the voices—all were snuffed out. Elizabeth fainted.

For one long, pure moment everything was calm and

dark. Her terrors dropped away. All was perfectly, delightfully still. Then her eyes flickered open.

Where am I? What happened? she thought. Half a dozen faces stared down at her. She recognized Lady Catherine and behind her, Kit Merrivale. He looked down at Elizabeth with eyes like stones . . . and smiled.

7

Maumesbury

sabella crept on her hands and knees to the doorway of the hermit's cell and stared out at the night. It was the end of the second day of waiting for Elizabeth. Wind whipped the tops of the trees, but the sky was clear. Stars glittered, and the warped disc of a moon shone high above the forest. Isabella sniffed the air, rich with the scent of old leaves and fresh earth. It was best to stay here, where people couldn't find her or be frightened by her. Best to remain with the other wild creatures—the deer that let her move among them, the boars, the bears, and the wolves.

Isabella rubbed her face, blinking away tears. It was no good. No matter how often she thought it through, no matter how safe she might be in the forest, she didn't want to be on her own any longer. She wanted a friend.

The crow people had provided company of a sort when she had lived with them. But she wasn't one of them. John, who had only begun to talk when they entered the shadow land, had been taken away from her. The hermit, Jerome, had been a good friend, but he was long gone. Isabella hungered to be with people like herself, for conversation by a warm fire. She had to find Elizabeth. She had to take the chance.

She stepped out of the cell, and moonlight striped her face. She shivered, though she didn't feel cold. The town lay to the north. It would be easy to find the way. Elizabeth's tracks still disturbed the forest litter, and towns were obvious to the eye, as well as the nose and ear. Like an animal, Isabella could see well enough in the dark, so she set off through the trees.

All was quiet. It was too dark for people to be about, but occasionally men hunted in the woods at night, poaching deer. Isabella could not afford to be careless. She emerged from the lair of trees and turned her face upward to test the air. She smelled no human scent, and all she could hear was the drip of moisture from the branches to the soft decaying fabric of the forest floor.

Keeping close to the tree line, she crept along a muddy track to the crossroads. Beyond the fields rose the town, houses heaped up the sides of the hill, and above it the broken walls of the old abbey. The town had grown since her last visit, but the abbey was greatly diminished. She frowned, shifting her weight from one foot to the other, trying to match up the new Maumesbury with the memory she had of the old.

Isabella lingered a moment. This was the turning point for her. Either she had to go back to the forest, or she had to commit herself to the open spaces of the fields and the dangers of the town. She took one tentative step along the road, then another and another. The wind rose, a sound like a sigh. The moonlight was very bright and cold, casting gray shadows behind the hedges. In one of the fields, half a dozen cows were dozing. They stirred as she passed, tossing their heads, shifting hooves on the muddy turf.

Creeping along the roadway, Isabella felt very small—as if the open sky threatened to swallow her up. Like a little beetle, she tried to hide in the shadows of the hedges. Finally, she reached Maumesbury. A stone bridge humped over the river at the town's feet, and a cobbled street rose from the bridge into the houses.

Where shall I go now? she wondered. *So many houses. Which one is Elizabeth's? How will I find her?*

She crossed the bridge. At the bottom of the hill were the poorer houses, many of them shacks of stick and thatch. Farther up, the houses were more substantial: rough stone or wattle and daub. The grandest houses of all stood on the top of the hill in the center of town. Isabella bit her lip. It seemed much chillier among these buildings than in the woods, and the smells nearly overwhelmed her—damp stone, cooked food, open sewers full of excrement, all overlaid with wood smoke from the fires that were keeping out the November cold.

She came to the marketplace and stared at the warm yellow light coming from the glass windows of the merchants' homes. Would she find Elizabeth here? She heard footsteps and spun around. On the other side of the marketplace, three dark figures were leaving an alehouse. Men, judging by the tone of their voices. One of them laughed, and Isabella held her breath. But they didn't see her. She crept up to one of the grand houses and pressed her face to the window.

A scene opened before her: a fire burning in a wide hearth . . . a family sitting together . . . a tapestry on the wall, a blur of blue and red beyond the thick glass. It seemed a happy scene to her, alone in the cold. She scanned the faces but didn't see Elizabeth. This was not the place.

Isabella slipped along a little alley and peered over the wooden fence that enclosed the yard of the next house. The back door was open, and she caught a glimpse of a kitchen. A servant woman had stepped out to throw rubbish into a pit at the end of the yard. She huffed and puffed, grumbling to herself.

Isabella thought hard. Dared she speak to the servant? Could she ask where Elizabeth lived? She touched her green face and the heavy rug of her hair. She might be chased away—or worse.

The servant bent over, tipping out the contents of her bucket. Then she straightened up, still grumbling, and headed back to the house.

Isabella took a deep breath. "Pardon me," she called out. "Could you tell me where I might find the home of the Dyer family?"

The woman halted. She turned her head, looking for the source of the question. "Who's there?" she asked suspiciously. "I can't see you. Who's there?"

Isabella stuck her head above the fence, so the woman could see her, but she tried to keep her face in the shadows.

The woman stared. "Who are you?" she said. "What are you doing out at this time of night?"

"I'm looking for my friend Elizabeth Dyer," Isabella said. "I know it's very late, but I need to find her."

"The Dyers?" the woman said. "What need have you of them? Who are you?" She screwed up her eyes and stepped closer, trying to make out who this visitor might be.

Isabella drew back. "Isabella Leland," she replied.

"Stand forward," the woman said. "Let me see you."

Inside the house someone called out. The servant sighed. "Silver Street. The big house with the red glass in the window." She gave a sniff. "The Dyers . . . godless, Catholic folk." She went inside, cutting off the dusting of light.

Isabella smiled. She remembered Silver Street very well. She skipped back along the alley and into the marketplace.

"Hey," a voice said. "Hey!"

A lantern was held aloft, and suddenly men were all around her. She panicked, trying to break away, and tripped over someone's rough-clothed leg. Voices started up, a shout of alarm.

"What *is* that?" said one. "Quick, catch it. Don't let it get away."

Isabella struggled to stand up, but the cobbles were slippery, and the men crowded around her. Their beery breath puffed warmly into the night air, and the sharp stink of their unwashed bodies was repellent. A hand seized her upper arm.

Isabella turned and bit hard. The hand was swiftly withdrawn.

"Little beast!" the man shouted. "Get your stick, Will. Whack it!"

A stick came down as Isabella wriggled on the ground—a painful blow on the shoulder. She cried out.

"Steady on, it's a girl," said another voice. "Don't hurt her."

"She bit me! Sorry sort of a girl."

The stick was withdrawn, but the men still stood around her, six or seven of them, in a tight circle. Someone raised the lantern, and as the light picked out her face and features, the voices died away.

Isabella looked from one man to another, seeking a way out. She jumped at the smallest one, trying to push him back, but another man grabbed her and wouldn't let go.

They all stared. "Look at the color of her," murmured her captor. "Come out of the forest, didn't she. Something unnatural."

"What shall we do?"

Isabella stood up straight. Her heart was hammering. How would she get away now? She took a deep breath and forced out the words. "My name is Isabella Leland," she said. "I have come to see my friend Elizabeth Dyer."

They looked at one another, then back at the green girl.

"She speaks funny," one said.

"The Dyers. Heretic people," said his neighbor.

"Let me go," Isabella said. "Let me pass." She was almost in tears now, choked with fear and frustration.

No one moved.

"Shall we take her to the parish priest?"

"Too late. Lock her up somewhere safe till morning. *Then* we'll take her to the priest. He'll know what to do."

Two men seized her, one to either side, pinching her bare arms with their strong, hard fingers. They disputed where the best place to keep her might be, then dragged her away from the marketplace and up a narrow lane, where one of the men owned a cooper's workshop.

"Put her in the storeroom at the back," he said. "I can bolt the door."

Isabella was thrown in without ceremony, and the bolt was drawn. She looked around. The storeroom was a tiny airless place with broken barrels and slices of wood heaped haphazardly about. She heard the men outside discuss who should keep guard during the night. Finally, there were goodnights and a departure. From the voices she could tell that two men were left behind.

Isabella sat among the barrels, her arms wrapped around her legs. She was utterly at the mercy of her captors, and men could be unspeakably cruel. Behind a locked, barred door in her mind, the memory of her mother's terrible fate rattled and called for attention. But Isabella turned away, as always. She would not look or listen. Not now, as she waited for daylight, and judgment.

8

The Parish Priest

sabella was too afraid to sleep. Curled among the broken barrels and splinters of wood, she strained to hear the men on the other side of the bolted door. She could make out their murmurs but not what they said. At last, when they fell silent—and asleep, she hoped—she began to look for a way out. She pressed against the door, feeling for a weakness in the wood. She scraped at the walls and even poked at the roof space. But the door refused to budge, and the old walls and muddy thatch were solid. So she closed her eyes and thought of the crow people, sending a call for their help, though she had little faith they would hear. She was too far away from the woods and springs where they could be summoned, where they could move easily from realm to realm.

Around and around the tiny space Isabella went like an animal in a cage. Charged with fear, her body longed for action—to fight or run—and whenever she tried to sleep, she just felt more awake and more afraid. So she shuffled and turned and paced within the confines of her little prison till her body was so tired it hurt.

Finally, the town around her began to stir. Isabella could hear horses shifting and stamping their feet in stalls nearby. A cockerel crowed far away, then another in the middle of the town, perhaps from someone's backyard. A dog barked. The first light leaked into the cooper's workshop and beneath the bolted door. From outside in the street came the tread of boots, the sound of voices. Then, closer to hand, Isabella heard her guards begin to wake and stir. Their voices were hard and loud, and they sounded nervous, wondering, perhaps—sober and in the clear light of day—what they had caught the night before.

"Shall we have a look?" one said. "Make sure it's still there?"

A moment's hesitation and murmuring.

The bolt drew back slowly. Isabella stood up straight, ready to escape if given a chance. The door opened a few inches, and a slice of a face became visible in the gap. A brown eye, a bearded cheek. The eye blinked, and the door closed again quickly.

"No doubt about it," the man said to his companion. "Green as moss. A goblin girl from the forest."

More waiting. Isabella was thirsty now, and her head ached. At last, she heard other men arrive, though she couldn't work out from the voices how many there were. They sounded excited, shouting to be heard one over the other.

"Fetch the parish priest," one said. "Bring him here to see her. That's safer than taking her to him. Besides, we don't want everyone else to know, coming here to take a peek."

More arguments. Then finally one of them left to fetch

the priest. While they waited, the men broke bread to share among themselves. The scent leaked into the storeroom, making Isabella's mouth water.

At last the parish priest arrived. Isabella heard him from some way off, grumbling in a loud voice along the street. Evidently, the men had gotten him out of bed. He had hurried his breakfast and obviously didn't believe what they had to tell him. The men's voices died away when the priest stepped into the workshop.

"Come along," she heard the priest say briskly. "Let's see what you have. Wasting my time like this. Your creature had better be real."

The men replied in lowered voices, deferring to the parish priest as though they were his children.

Helpless, Isabella shrank to the rear of the storeroom till staves of wood pressed into her back. The bolt was drawn once more, and the door swung wide open. Early-morning light streaked the dim room, and Isabella covered her face with her hands. She heard the priest gasp. Slowly she peered through her fingers.

The scene revealed itself: a stout priest in a dark robe, surrounded by other men squeezed close together to catch a glimpse—these dozen faces all turned toward her. The priest crossed himself and crossed himself again. They were silent for a few moments, all of them, as though even the men who had caught her in the marketplace couldn't quite believe their eyes.

The priest swallowed. Shaken out of his composure, he tried to pull himself together. "Can she speak?" he asked abruptly.

"She spoke last night. Gave us her name."

The priest leaned toward her and held out a hand. "Good day," he said gently. "What's your name?"

Isabella shook her head, and the rug of draggled hair fell over her shoulders. She peered at him through her fingers.

"Tell me who you are," the priest said. "Come along, now."

Isabella didn't know what to do. There had been priests before, and they had not been kind. However, Jerome had fed her and befriended her and done her a great service. She shook her head again, a quick, animal movement, like a dog with a gnat in its ear.

"Speak to me," the priest coaxed. He turned his head to the men, all gawping at Isabella. "Has she been given food?" he asked. "Anything to drink?"

The men looked away, as if each expected another to make a reply and take the blame. "No, no," one finally said. And another ran off quickly to pick up the remnants of their breakfast of bread and small beer.

"Give it to me, give it to me," the priest snapped impatiently. He snatched the crust and held it out to Isabella. "Are you hungry?" he asked. "It is good bread."

Isabella reached out to take the crust, but at the final moment, the priest drew it away from her. "Tell me your name," he said. "Then you may have the bread."

Isabella retreated again, shifting her weight from one leg to the other, left to right, right to left. She was trapped now, between anxiety and hunger. She could smell the bread, sweet and warm, and she licked her lips.

"Isabella Leland," she said. "My name is Isabella Leland."

The priest nodded. She stretched out her hand again for the crust, but he held on to it. "How long have you been in the forest?" he asked.

Isabella stared at him. How long? She had no idea. Time with the crow people didn't count as time in the so-many-Sundays sense. She couldn't answer.

The priest shrugged. He handed over the crust, and Isabella crammed it into her mouth. Then he turned to the men. "Remarkable," he said. "You were right to fetch me."

The men relaxed and nodded, whispering to one another. A sense of excitement rose. "What do you think she is?" one asked the priest. "A faerie girl? Look at the color of her. A green girl."

The priest shook his head. "No," he said. "Nothing un-natural. She's been living in the forest."

"Reared by wolves," the man suggested.

"Like Romulus and Remus?" the priest responded. "Then how did she learn to speak? Clearly she's been living on her own for some time. For years, probably. But she is re-markable, for all that, because she has survived."

"But the color!" another man said, pointing to Isabella's face. He reached out with a grimy hand to touch her cheek, but she drew away, as though his fingers would scald.

"I think the color would wash away in time," the priest mused. He rubbed his own very clean, soft hands together.

Someone offered Isabella a leather bottle. She took it gin-gerly. The bottle stank of small beer, ripe and fruity, and of the accumulated sweat from the man's hand. His spittle glittered on the neck. Isabella held the bottle for a moment or two, wondering if her thirst outweighed her sense of revulsion. Slowly she raised the bottle and tipped a drop of the contents into her mouth. It was foul stuff, and although her mouth seemed to soak up the liquid before she had even swallowed, the taste made her cough and gag.

The men laughed to see her reaction to the beer, but the priest frowned and silenced them with a little gesture of his hand.

Isabella held out the bottle, wanting to be rid of it, looking from one face to another.

The man took his bottle back. "What shall we do with her?" he asked, grinning and leering at Isabella.

"We must find her somewhere suitable to stay," the priest said. "We do not know how she will behave. She looks"—he wrinkled his nose—"and smells like an animal. But I have an idea. I will need a horse and rider to take a message. In the meantime, give her some milk to drink and more food." He stared at Isabella one last time, drinking her in with his eyes, committing the very sight of her to memory. He nodded, with some satisfaction. Then he turned away. The door was closed and bolted.

Now that the threat had temporarily abated, Isabella relaxed a little. She was so tired, and her nerves were strung out after the long night. She curled up tightly on the floor . . . closed her eyes. Sleep drowned her, as if she'd fallen into a deep black well. Yet she woke up as the door opened. A hand presented a rough wooden platter with bread and cheese and a bowl of milk, still warm—and withdrew. Isabella ate and drank till her stomach felt as tight as a drum. Then she sank into sleep once more, swallowed up, exhausted.

Sometime later the door opened yet again, the bolt making a great noise. Isabella jumped, scrambled to her feet. Another visitor?

Lavender perfume billowed into the room in a cloud. Isabella saw a gold ring glinting on a woman's gloved finger . . . a fine dress . . . and an oval face with a high forehead, curls of dark red hair pinned back under a soft black cap. She took a deep breath, her heart beating hard. Had the crow people sent this woman to set her free?

No, she thought, shaking her head. The lady was beautiful and finely dressed. But she wasn't really like the faeries. Beneath the perfume, Isabella sensed the familiar sour smell of mortal flesh.

Beside the fine lady stood a young man dressed in mud-splashed leather and velvet. His dark hair hung to his shoulders. He wore a pearl earring and carried a riding crop in one hand. The man stepped forward as though to grab Isabella, but she scurried back to the wall, evading his grip.

"Leave her!" the woman said.

The young man glowered at the reprimand, then leaned back on his heels, smirking.

Isabella raised her face cautiously, peering at the young man in case he should try to grab her again. Then the lady spoke, more gently now. "Isabella," she said. "They told me that is your name. Isabella Leland. Will you speak to me? I am Lady Catherine. I want to take you to my house. We have room for you there and can care for you."

Isabella trembled. The lady's tone of voice appealed to her, but she was suspicious. She couldn't trust anyone.

Instinctively, she drew back her lips and snarled. The sound was so wolflike, the lady gasped. The young man stepped forward, riding crop raised, ready to strike. Isabella regarded him directly and snarled again.

"Shall we see if she bites?" the man said.

"No," Lady Catherine said, nudging him aside. "You're frightening her, can't you see?" She stretched out her hand to Isabella, the small, white-gloved fingers reaching for Isabella's rough, mottled green ones.

"Come, Isabella," Lady Catherine said. "I shan't hurt you. I have a place where you can stay."

Isabella stared at the hand now opened to her. She knew she might face the harder fists of the man if she didn't do as she was told. She didn't want to stay in the cooper's storeroom for a minute longer, and maybe the chance for escape would come later. She took the white hand in her own green one and squeezed the lady's fingers.

"Come along," Lady Catherine said. She turned to reveal a crowd gathered in the room, with the parish priest at the front, nodding graciously. The crowd parted before them, leaving a pathway through the workshop to the open door. Two saddled horses were tethered outside. A third was harnessed to a low cart, a driver holding its reins. The lady led Isabella to the cart and gestured to her to climb up. When Isabella was safely on board, the young man helped Lady Catherine onto her horse, where she sat sidesaddle, tucking her skirts decorously about her.

"Don't be afraid," Lady Catherine said. "I shall ride right beside you, Isabella. We'll be home soon. Be glad! You shall be well cared for."

Beside her the young man sneered, as if scornful of the kindness Lady Catherine was lavishing on Isabella. But he made no comment.

Apparently, word of the green girl had spread, for quite a crowd had gathered around the cart and the lady on her horse. Everyone stared at Isabella, her moss-colored skin and pelt of hair. The women whispered to one another. One or two of the onlookers dared themselves to touch her, reaching out their hands, but the driver shooed them away. He flicked the reins on the horse's rump, and the cart lumbered off, following the riders over the muddy cobbled streets to the marketplace, down the hill, and out of the town.

Both Lady Catherine and her companion kept a close eye on Isabella as they traveled. In the distance Isabella saw the woods, dark and welcoming, and she considered jumping from the cart, trying to flee to her old home. She knew that the man on the horse would pursue her, and though she was afraid of his fists and riding crop, she thought she could dodge him. But something stopped her from escaping: she simply didn't want to be alone anymore. The crow people had left her behind, dumping her in the forest and flying away like swallows at the end of summer. It was possible they would come back again, as they had before. But Isabella wasn't sure she wanted to return to them, to be treated like a toy to be picked up and tossed aside as it pleased them.

She remained in the cart.

9

The Green Girl

lizabeth woke, struggling for breath. The darkness seemed heavy, as though it were pressing on her chest and limbs as she tried to move. For a few moments her mind was blank; she couldn't remember where she was or why she was so afraid. Her thoughts whirled. She couldn't see anything. Then something shifted beside her, with a grunt and a tug on the blanket covering them both, and everything fell into place. She was lying beside the cook in the manor at Spirit Hill, and she feared her beloved family was in great danger.

She forced herself to take a deep breath . . . once, twice. The panic that froze her thoughts would not help her face the peril that threatened them. She remembered Thomas Montford telling her how he said how-do-you-do to his fears and then put them behind him. But her fears were like wild dogs, constantly biting and worrying and tugging and gnawing. How could she put them to one side? She took another deep breath, closed her eyes, and tried to pray.

I am not alone, she thought. *God is with me, if I open my heart to him, and his love will take the place of the fear.* In her mind she recited the Pater Noster and the Ave Maria, concentrating on the words to calm herself. Then, trying to assess the danger she faced and what she could do about it, she went over the events of the previous evening one by one. . . .

When Elizabeth had revived from her faint, Lady Catherine fussed and had the servants help Elizabeth to the next room, away from the fire, to recover. She blamed the heat and smoke for Elizabeth's fainting spell and shooed the others off to allow her space and air. But Elizabeth saw that Merrivale had a curiously cold smile on his face, and she was horrified. Had she given herself away? Had Merrivale understood why the conversation had frightened her so much?

Even after most of the household had retired to bed, Lady Catherine stayed up, talking with Merrivale. Elizabeth lay down beside the cook, unable to sleep or close her eyes, fearing what Merrivale might say. But she must have slept for a short while, because the next thing she knew, Lady Catherine was standing over her with a candle in her hand. She looked tired in the dim light, and her hair had come loose from her cap.

"Wake up, Elizabeth," Lady Catherine said. "I need you to help me undress. Come to my chamber."

Elizabeth hurriedly got to her feet and, dressed in her white shift, followed Lady Catherine up the stairs to her chamber. A chilly draft blew along the corridor, nipping at Elizabeth's ankles. The house was silent, except for the sound of Lady Catherine's shoes and Elizabeth's bare feet. The solitary candle sent wavering shadows along the floorboards.

Lady Catherine closed the door behind them and set the candle down on her little table. She drew the curtains. "Unfasten the dress," she said.

As Elizabeth's fingers fumbled with the buttons and ties, Lady Catherine sighed. "You will have to stay here at Spirit Hill," she said.

Elizabeth's fingers stopped altogether. "What?" she said faintly.

"Kit Merrivale is a priest hunter," Lady Catherine said, keeping her voice low. "Your family has come under suspicion. It is likely your mother will be arrested and questioned. I am very fond of you, Elizabeth. Your company has been a gift for me, stuck here among so many ignorant and insensitive country people. I appreciate that you are only a child, that you have been obliged to follow the religious path your family set down for you, and I wish to protect you if I can. Kit is a good man, but he has a duty to the queen and to England."

Elizabeth's mouth felt numb, and when she spoke, her voice sounded odd. "Why has my family come under suspicion?" she asked. "What are we supposed to have done?"

"A heretic priest, come from Douai, has fled Oxford, where he celebrated Mass in secret for Catholic students. Several of them have been arrested and questioned, and their evidence suggests that this traitor priest was heading for Maumesbury."

Elizabeth swallowed hard, and Lady Catherine turned to face her. "You've been a loyal friend to me," she said. "You are bright and clever and friendly, and I have come to love you." She looked into Elizabeth's face as though she was searching for something, and Elizabeth waited for the inevitable question, for Lady Catherine to ask if she knew the whereabouts of the priest. But Lady Catherine didn't ask. Perhaps she already knew the answer.

"I don't wish to see you caught up in this," Lady Catherine went on. "I understand your loyalties to your family and their faith, but I want you to stay here with me—for your own safety."

Elizabeth barely heard these words. Her mind was a whirl of images—men coming for her mother and sister, the priest being dragged off for torture and execution. She rocked on her feet, afraid she would faint again.

"Elizabeth? Elizabeth, are you listening to me?" Lady Catherine said. "Kit is an honorable man, and I think"—a smile strayed across her face—"that I have some influence over him. He will listen to me. Stay close to me. Stay at Spirit Hill."

In the morning, Elizabeth lay beside the hot, smelly cook and racked her brain. She was forbidden to leave the house, and her family was in danger. What could she do? How could she warn them?

She got up at the same time as the cook and dressed in the half-light. In the kitchen, the sleepy servants revived the fire, cleaned up from the dinner of the night before, and prepared a breakfast. The lord's men got up late, nursing headaches and standing about in the warmth of the kitchen. Three lean dogs cringed at their feet or else growled and scrabbled for scraps thrown down. She suspected the men were bored in the quiet countryside.

Doubtless they wished they were at court with their master instead.

The other servants gave her sidelong glances, but nobody spoke to her except once, to tell her that Lady Catherine and Kit Merrivale had gone out early on their horses. So Elizabeth stayed in the kitchen.

The cook was elbow-deep in a wooden tub of lamb's entrails, the air perfumed with the hard-iron odor of liver. "May I help?" Elizabeth asked. "I prepare food at home for my mother."

The cook's arms were red to the elbow, streaked with dark blood. A pearl of moisture hung from her nose, which she wiped with the back of her hand. Now the tip of her nose was smudged with red, and snot mingled with the blood on her hand. She turned to stare at Elizabeth. "This is kitchen work. Not for you, Dyer," she said. "Go and wait for the lady. You're nothing to do with me."

"Where shall I wait?" Elizabeth asked.

But the cook had turned away from her and merely shrugged, plunging her arms back into the tub.

Helpless, Elizabeth turned and slowly made her way to Lady Catherine's empty room, where a little maid, a couple of years younger than Elizabeth, was sweeping the hearth. Clouds of ash puffed up as she shoveled the cold remains of the fire into a basket. She coughed, waving away the dust with her hand. Then she turned and grinned at Elizabeth, her face gray with soot.

"You're the Catholic girl, Elizabeth Dyer, aren't you?" she said.

Elizabeth nodded.

"Everyone is talking about you," the girl continued brightly. She put down the brush and basket and wiped her eyes with her fingertips. "They say the lady's keeping you here because she feels sorry for you." She stared at Elizabeth, as though she was deciding for herself if Elizabeth merited pity.

"What's your name?" Elizabeth asked.

"Deb. Deb Glover," the girl replied. "Are you really a Catholic? That means you'll go to hell."

Elizabeth shrugged uneasily. "Yes, I'm a Catholic," she said.

They didn't speak further, because Deb was called away to tend to another fire. Alone, worn out by anxiety and homesickness, Elizabeth sat by the empty hearth. She dozed then . . . and woke to the sound of doors banging, loud voices calling, and some kind of dispute taking place in the long hall. One of the dogs barked. A ripple of excitement, a quiver of expectation flowed through the household. Elizabeth could detect it, even sitting alone in Lady Catherine's chamber. But she was afraid to move. Had something terrible happened?

The door burst open. It was Deb Glover, a huge grin on her face. She was obviously dying to tell the news to someone—to anyone. "Come and see," she panted, out of breath from running up the stairs. "They've caught a faerie. Out in the woods. They've brought it here. It's bright green like a cabbage, with a wolf's coat and sharp teeth and wings. It's the strangest thing! They've locked it in the stables so it won't escape, and the men have got sticks—in case it attacks. Come on, come and see."

Elizabeth stood up, and the floor seemed to plunge beneath her feet. Isabella! It *had* to be Isabella they had captured. What would they do to her? Had they hurt her?

Deb was already off again, running down the stairs. Elizabeth steadied herself, then hurried out of the house toward the stables. The cook came running heavily from the kitchen, wiping her hands on her apron. Others followed. The entire house was agog.

"This way!" Deb called, prancing ahead, eyes alight.

Elizabeth shivered in the bitter cold. She looked across the fields, and for an instant she considered taking advantage of the excitement at the manor and running away, back to the town, to warn her mother and the priest. But wouldn't that simply confirm Merrivale's suspicions? How much did he really know? Was he setting her some kind of test, to see what she would do? She couldn't take the chance. There had to be another way to warn her family, a way that was secret and circumspect.

The stables stood in a courtyard behind the house. They were solid and stone-built, like the manor itself. It seemed the entire household was crowded around the entrance, fighting to get through the door. The men were at the front, pushing the others out of the way. Deb was at the back, hopping up and down like a little bird, trying in vain to see over shoulders.

"Stop pushing!" Kit Merrivale shouted the order.

At the sound of his voice, the tight bunch of bodies at the stable door began to loosen and back away. Elizabeth wondered why they all, even Lord Cecil's men, deferred to him—this young upstart who had arrived only two days before.

But it was the men who were allowed to see the faerie first, while the lesser servants waited outside.

Elizabeth sidled up to Deb. "Please tell me about the faerie," she said.

Deb stood straight, full of importance at being the bearer of news. "They say it came from the woods," she whispered. "Some men caught it in the town late last night. I expect it was up to some wickedness." She made a curious little gesture, bunching her fist and sticking her thumb through her fingers—a sign of protection against the evil eye.

The men took a long time surveying the faerie. Waiting outside, the servants could hear their voices, the occasional burst of laughter or heated exclamation. At last the men emerged, shaking their heads, animated and excited. Then the dozen or so servants swarmed in to see the captive creature.

Elizabeth hung back at first. She was afraid to see Isabella. Had they beaten her? Was she hurt? And what would Isabella do if she saw Elizabeth? Finally, she crept in behind everyone else.

Inside the long, low building, the horses were stabled in stalls separated by wooden panels. The floor was bedded with straw, and the air was sweet—the scent of long-gone summer preserved in the dried meadow grass. After the wait in the bitterly cold yard, the stables felt warm.

Deb pushed her way in, bobbing up and down to get a better view. "It's true!" she cried in her high, shrill voice. "It's true. The faerie's green!" She made the little gesture again, covertly; then she added in a disappointed tone, "But it hasn't got wings. They said it had wings."

The other servants craned their necks to see. Elizabeth crept forward, keeping herself obscured by the cram of bodies. She peeped through a gap in the planks of the stall—and saw Isabella.

The wild girl crouched in the corner, pressed against the stone wall, on a fresh mound of straw. A platter of bread and cheese waited on the floor beside her, but this appeared to be untouched. Elizabeth could make out the rise and fall of Isabella's body as she breathed. How green she looked. How small, too, as though she had shrunk, once away from the forest.

"It's a girl," one of the women said. "Poor thing. It's only a girl."

"But look at the color of her," another said. "That's not like any girl I've ever seen. It isn't natural."

"Come from under the hills," one of the older men piped up. "A goblin girl. One of the faerie people."

Isabella looked up, her attention snagged by the man's last words, and her eyes flared. A murmur rose from the gathering.

"You're right," the first woman remarked. "She knows what you said."

But Isabella's interest didn't last. The light seemed to fade from her eyes, and she stared straight ahead, indifferent to them all.

"Come up here, Elizabeth. Come and see."

Deb's voice was loud, and at the mention of Elizabeth's name, Isabella looked up again.

"Come on," Deb insisted. "You can't see properly from there. Don't be afraid! She won't hurt you."

Elizabeth sighed. She took a deep breath and stood up, revealing herself to the green girl. They gazed at each other one long moment. And in that moment, Elizabeth tried to convey her sense of failure, her continued loyalty, and an apology. *I'll come back,* she promised silently. *I'll help you escape, Isabella. I want to be your friend.*

Did Isabella understand? It was hard to know. She said nothing and gave no sign that she knew Elizabeth. Instead, she stared straight ahead again, apparently lost in thoughts faraway.

Finally, Lady Catherine arrived and shooed everyone out like so many chickens—all except Elizabeth. "What do you think?" she asked, nodding to the green girl.

Elizabeth swallowed, not wanting to give anything away but afraid to deceive Lady Catherine about her relationship with Isabella. "She is a remarkable creature," she said. "What will happen to her now?"

"I think we should take care of her. She needs to be cleaned and made respectable again, brought back into Christian company."

"Do you think she is a goblin or a boggart or something from under the hills, like the men said?" Elizabeth asked, careful not to stare at Isabella.

"No," replied Lady Catherine. "Perhaps she has simply been living alone in the woods for a long time. She is an unusual creature nonetheless, and I don't know what to make of her. She can speak well enough and told me her name is Isabella. Perhaps she will tell us her history in her own good time."

At the mention of her name, Isabella blinked and shifted

on the straw. Something clinked when she moved . . . a chain, one end fastened to a manacle about her wrist, the other to an iron hoop on the wall.

Elizabeth gasped.

"It's for her own good, Elizabeth," Lady Catherine said. "For her protection, you understand. She might not realize what is best for her yet. And if she escaped, she might be misunderstood and badly treated. She will only be chained until we know we can trust her to stay with us."

Elizabeth nodded, but her heart was heavy.

Lady Catherine shivered and tucked her fur collar more tightly about her neck. "Isabella doesn't seem to feel the cold as we do," she said. "But she will need a blanket, even so. I'll have one brought out to her. Come along now. It is time for us to eat."

10

Friends

In the afternoon Kit Merrivale ordered his servant to saddle his horse and then rode off alone beneath a clear sky. From a window, Lady Catherine and Elizabeth watched him trot down the drive. He turned and waved his hat in farewell. Lady Catherine smiled and lifted her hand in reply.

Elizabeth did not respond. Lady Catherine wouldn't tell her why Merrivale had to leave or where he was going, and Elizabeth suspected the worst. He was following the trail of the Oxford priest, and this trail would surely lead him to the only Catholic household in Maumesbury, her home in Silver Street. She shivered and rubbed her arms.

Lady Catherine, obviously torn between her affection for her companion and her infatuation with the young gallant from court, patted Elizabeth on the shoulder. "Don't worry," she said. "You're safe. I'm sure everything will be fine."

These words must have sounded as hollow to her as they did to Elizabeth, because she patted Elizabeth again, a little harder, and turned away. "I'm going to rest," she said briskly. "I'll send for you later."

Elizabeth remained at the window, watching Merrivale disappear down the long, gentle slope of Spirit Hill. In the distance, Maumesbury rose from the bleached, level landscape like a clenched fist. When she could no longer see him, she turned away, too.

Downstairs, the servants were busy preparing another lavish dinner to impress the London guest. The atmosphere in the kitchen was warm, the women trading gossip and jokes. A brace of pheasants hung from a hook near the door, the dead, stiff wings still glowing with feathers of red and gold. Mud and vegetable peelings mingled on the floor. The stinging perfume of cloves and nutmeg threaded through the pervading atmosphere of pig's blood and smoke.

No one acknowledged Elizabeth when she stepped into the room. Despite the rigid hierarchy the servants maintained and the insults they traded freely among themselves, they were a close family, and Elizabeth, a Catholic and an outsider, was not part of it.

Elizabeth noticed that Deb Glover, busy gutting fish, was sniffing and wiping her eyes. Doubtless she'd had another scolding from the cook. Poor Deb was the lowest of low among the female servants. Still, Elizabeth envied her, envied that she had nothing more to worry about than the cook's bad temper. It would be pleasant to belong, Elizabeth thought, to know what was expected and to be safe.

Nobody stopped her as she edged her way to the back door. She stepped into the fresh, chilly November sunshine—then waited, just outside, to hear what the servants might say.

There was a moment's silence; then someone muttered, "I don't like her creeping around."

"Don't know why the lady has to take in a papist," someone else responded. "Did you see the girl faint when the talk turned to heretics? It's not right. They side with the Spanish, those Catholics. We'll be overrun. None of us is safe. And we have to put up with a spy in the house."

"I have to share a bed with her," chimed in the cook. "What do you think about that?"

Elizabeth stepped away, not wanting to hear more. The servants' venom was a shock. Did they hate her so much? She imagined their poisonous feelings fogging the house and choking her, and she longed to be home with her family. Many people in town treated her with suspicion, but not everyone. And at least there she had her loved ones to shore up her morale against any surly comments. Here she was alone.

Elizabeth headed for the stables, looked around to make sure that no one was watching, and then opened the door. Isabella sat up straight when she stepped inside. Elizabeth swallowed nervously. "Isabella," she said. "It's me, Elizabeth."

Isabella nodded. "Yes."

"I'm sorry they chained you up."

"It doesn't matter," said Isabella. She folded her hand, thumb to little finger, compressing the bones together. The manacle slid off easily.

Elizabeth stared. "How can you do that?" she asked. "And why do you stay chained up if you can escape? Who are you, Isabella?"

Isabella asked her own question. "I waited for you in the wood; why didn't you come back?"

"I couldn't!" Elizabeth said. "I wanted to, but I had to come here to wait on Lady Catherine, and she wouldn't let me go home, and I was thinking about you and worrying, and now my family is in terrible danger, and I can't warn them, and everything is going wrong." She dipped her head, helpless tears flooding her eyes and dripping down her cheeks.

Isabella stepped toward her and hesitantly held out a hand. Elizabeth, blinded by tears, didn't see the gesture, so Isabella stretched out her arms. With only the slightest hesitation, Elizabeth stepped into the stall, and they held each other tight, Elizabeth's wet cheek on Isabella's shoulder.

Finally, Elizabeth pulled away, and the two girls sank onto the straw to sit side by side, backs pressed against the wooden partition. Nearby, the horses tugged at racks of hay. The sound of their munching was soothing. Elizabeth wiped her face on her sleeve.

"When I saw you in the wood, you gave me your food," Isabella said. "It's been such a long time since anyone was kind to me. That's why I went to town. I was looking for you. Was I right? Did I understand properly? Will you be my friend, Elizabeth?" Isabella hesitated, then went on. "I've never had a friend before. I had my mother and my little brother, John, but no one ever wanted to be my friend."

"I've never had a friend, either," Elizabeth said. "My family is Catholic. Nobody wants to associate with me, except Lady Catherine, and that is out of pity and because I'm her servant." She looked sideways at Isabella, wondering if

Isabella would change her mind about their friendship, now that she knew Elizabeth's faith. But Isabella didn't pull away. She just looked puzzled.

"What are the others, if they're not Catholic?" she asked. "I thought everyone was a Catholic."

"That changed years ago, when King Henry broke with the Pope and made himself head of the Church of England," said Elizabeth. She was agog to think Isabella didn't know this. How much of her life had the girl spent with the beasts in the forest?

But the green girl was obviously thinking about something else, winding herself up to speak. She took a deep, ragged breath. "Elizabeth," she said. "You asked me who I am. Well, I am almost afraid to tell you, because either you will think I'm mad, or, worse, you will think I'm something terrible."

Elizabeth shook her head. "I will never think you are terrible," she said. "I know already that you are something strange. The way you move and look. The way you don't feel the cold."

Isabella sighed again. "Who is King of England now? What is the year?" she asked.

The questions took Elizabeth aback. "King?" she said. "We have no king. England is ruled by Queen Elizabeth." She looked into the green girl's face. "You didn't know this?"

"Listen to me, Elizabeth. Please listen. I used to live in a cottage on the edge of the forest, and Henry the Third was king. I saw him once. He came to Maumesbury to visit William of Cullerne, the abbot at the monastery, in the year

1239. Then my mother sent John and me into the shadow land. She gave us to the crow people and asked them to care for us. From time to time I returned to the ordinary world because I missed it, because I belong here. But it has never been safe for me to stay long."

Elizabeth stared at Isabella, her mouth slightly open. She frowned and, without realizing what she was doing, moved slightly away. Slowly, Isabella's words sank in, but nothing made sense. "It is the year of Our Lord 1586," she said. "Who are the crow people?"

Isabella swallowed. "They have many names," she said. "Boggarts. Faeries. The Old Ones."

Elizabeth went cold. "Faeries?" she said. "You have lived with the faeries for more than three hundred years? That is what you're saying?"

Isabella's face seemed to close up, and Elizabeth realized how cold her voice had become. Confusion and fear wrestled inside her. She wanted to reassure Isabella, but something held her back. Could this be the truth? There were old stories about the forest, and years before, three women had been hanged for practicing witchcraft after having confessed, under torture, to cavorting with demons and spirits in the wood. The story had been much embellished over time and was often repeated to children to frighten them into behaving. Elizabeth didn't know how much truth survived in the tale, but few townspeople liked to stray alone in the woods.

What did Elizabeth believe? Judging by Isabella's green skin and the effortless way she had freed herself from an iron manacle, she had no trouble surmising that the girl possessed an unholy power. For God had made man and the heavenly host, but the unclean spirits of the wood drew their magic from another source.

"Devils," Elizabeth whispered. "Magic, sorcery—it is the work of the devil." Should she tell Thomas Montford, for the sake of Isabella's soul? The girl should be confessed and given absolution, her sins wiped away. Otherwise, she would be damned; she would tumble into the eternal fire with Satan, to face unending punishment.

Perhaps sensing her thoughts, Isabella turned away from Elizabeth. "Do you think I'm evil? Do you think I'm something wicked because I'm not like you?" she asked. "Yet you say that people think you're bad because you don't believe the same things they believe. Explain to me why they don't like you."

Elizabeth took a deep breath. Where to begin? Slowly she explained about the Reformation, how Queen Elizabeth's father, Henry the Eighth, had torn down Maumesbury Abbey and established the Church of England; how his elder daughter, Mary, had restored Catholicism for a few brief years; and how his second daughter, Elizabeth, had reinstated the Church of England upon ascending the throne. She explained the fate of heretics and the crippling fines her family paid for their refusal to attend church services. It was a long, complicated story, and some way through this rambling account, she realized that she had lost Isabella.

The green girl shook her head. "It is very hard to understand."

Elizabeth was torn. She longed to tell Isabella about Thomas and to ask for her help. But revealing this secret seemed too risky, even though Isabella had just placed her life in Elizabeth's hands. The story she had told was enough to have her tried and executed for witchcraft.

Elizabeth was also wary. After so many years of fear and secrecy, she couldn't help wondering if this was all a trick. What if Isabella was in league with the priest hunter?

"I don't know what to think," she said at last. "Nothing makes sense. Why are you green, Isabella? Is this an enchantment?"

"I think the coloring is part of my faerie self, and I've spent so long in the shadow land, it has become a part of my earthly body as well."

"And the way you move? Is that part of your faerie self?"

"Yes. And the way I sense things, too. I think if I stayed here in the mortal world a long time, the color would fade, and I would become ordinary again. Maybe we all have a self in the faerie land, but mostly we aren't aware of it—except, perhaps, in those odd moments when everything seems particularly bright and the world shines, or a shadow makes you shiver for no reason."

Elizabeth nodded. She knew those feelings.

"When you live in the shadow land," Isabella went on, "you leave a part of your earthly body behind—a handful of bones, a hank of hair or a skull, or your fingernails and toenails. These mortal remains bind you to the place you belong."

Elizabeth went pale. This talk of other selves, of toenails and markers of bone, conjured up horrible images of witchcraft.

Isabella took hold of her hands. "Look at me," she said. "How do I know you're not evil because you're a Catholic and all the others are—whatever they are now? *They* believe you're evil. How do I know whether that's true?"

Elizabeth stared at Isabella, longing to trust her.

"Look at me, Elizabeth. In my time everyone was a Catholic, because there was only one church, but I was different because of the shadow land, and so I was mistrusted. Don't let your mind be clouded by what other people have told you. Judge me with your heart."

Elizabeth looked into Isabella's clear eyes, studied her bright, vulnerable face. "I don't think you're evil," she whispered. "Of course I don't. God help me, I can feel how good you are. It gives me strength just to talk with you, to hold your hand."

A smile stole across Isabella's face, and Elizabeth began to smile as well.

"Then we are friends," Isabella said. "Tell me what has happened, and I will help."

Elizabeth nodded. She had made her decision. "I will help you, too," she said.

11

Priest Hunters

he two girls talked for a long time, until the November afternoon deepened and darkness crept over the fields. When Elizabeth realized how late it had become, she worried she would be missed in the house. She gave Isabella one final embrace and pressed her worn wooden rosary beads into the green girl's hand. Then she hurried away.

Isabella watched her through the window, the pale form running across the yard and through a door into the house. She waited another hour or so and ate the food she had been given. Then she left the stable herself, heading away from the manor and back to the town.

She covered the ground swiftly, running fast and low, her feet barely leaving an impression. As she crossed the fields, she startled some sheep, and they jumped to their feet and hurtled away. Isabella laughed out loud. Inspired by her purpose, warmed by Elizabeth's offered friendship and the real evidence of her trust, she felt vital and alive. She enjoyed the sensation of blood moving through her limbs and the moist earth compacting under her bare feet. She was afraid, yes, but for the moment, the fear had transformed itself into energy, and she felt exhilarated.

Elizabeth had explained where her house was on Silver Street, and Isabella, moving like a wolf, loped over the bridge and up the cobbled hill into the town. She found the house marked by the stained-glass panel in the front window. Shadowlike, slinking, she made her way to the back door and knocked gently, careful to keep to the darkness.

The door swung open, and an elderly woman holding a candle peered out. "Who's there?" she asked, her voice full of suspicion.

"Mary?" Isabella said. "Are you Mary? Don't be afraid. I have a message from Elizabeth. I need to speak to her mother."

"Who is it?" A second anxious voice, another woman.

Isabella crept forward, so the wavering candlelight fell upon her. The two women gasped, and Mary drew back, crossing herself quickly.

"Elizabeth sent me," Isabella said. "Please—please let me in. I need to speak to you."

Mary shook her head violently. "Don't listen, Mistress," she said. "It's a trick. Send the creature away."

Isabella's heart sank. She had to convince them. "Please," she said. "For Elizabeth's sake. I'm her friend. She sent me to you from the manor."

"Is she in trouble?" Jane asked, stepping forward suddenly. "What's happened to her? Why have they kept her there? What is it?"

"Elizabeth is fine," Isabella said. She shifted forward,

toward the door. "She said to give you this so you would believe me." Isabella held out the rosary.

Elizabeth's mother took the string of beads. She held it on her palm, staring. Then she nodded. "Come inside," she said. "Quickly, now."

Mary shook her head, but she allowed Isabella to pass by; then she shut and locked the door behind her.

Isabella knew the women would see her more clearly in the light from the fire in the kitchen hearth. She pushed the mat of hair back over her shoulders, then hid her long-nailed hands behind her back. Jane Dyer and the housekeeper stared, but Isabella began to speak. She didn't have much time.

"Elizabeth said to warn you that the priest is in danger. Some of the others from Oxford have been captured and examined. She said Walsingham had taken them to the tower, and a plot had been discovered. She is afraid they will have confessed under torture and may have named Thomas Montford and your son. And now there is a priest hunter staying at the manor. A man called Kit Merrivale." Isabella took a deep breath. Had she remembered everything correctly? Would they believe her or suspect a trap? They might think the rosary was nothing more than a trick, for Elizabeth could have been arrested and searched and the beads taken. The circle of suspicion and secrecy was dizzying.

Jane raised her hand to her mouth, her eyes bright with tears. "What shall we do?" she moaned. "What shall we do? What shall we do?"

The housekeeper stepped forward and placed her hand on her mistress's arm. In the face of Jane's indecision, Mary made the choice. "I'll get the priest. He should speak to her," she said, gesturing to Isabella.

Jane nodded, the tears on her cheeks glittering. "My poor, poor Robert," she whispered. "What will become of him? Oh, if only Edward were home. If only I were not on my own, always on my own. And they've taken Elizabeth from me, too."

Mary hurried from the kitchen, and in a moment she returned with the priest. Isabella saw that he was well built and strong. His face was bearded. He looked at her directly, his eyes quick and clever. A man, she sensed, who would not crumble like Mistress Dyer, a man who would stand up to a challenge.

"What manner of creature are you?" he said.

"I—"

"Sir, she must be the goblin," Mary interrupted. "All day the town has buzzed with the news of it."

"The buzzing of the town is not my concern," he said. His voice was firm, but Isabella could detect no malice in it. The man simply wanted to get to the pith of the matter. Quickly she told him her name, that she had been living in the woods, and that she had a message from Elizabeth.

The priest stepped forward and seized her hand. He examined the green skin, the horny nails springing from her fingertips. He peered into her face and lifted her hair. Then he dropped her hand and stepped away.

"She's a girl, Mary. Neither more nor less," he said. "She needs to be washed and to have her hair and nails cut, that's all. Pay no attention to the superstitious fools in the town." He turned again to Isabella. "Now, tell me everything you know. How did you meet Elizabeth? What exactly did she tell you?"

Half an hour later Isabella slid from the rear door of the Dyers' house and began the journey back to the manor. She had to return before anyone discovered she was missing. But she was tired now.

Stars wheeled overhead as Isabella reached the bridge at the edge of town. She rested for a moment, staring at the black water that jostled and chattered over the stones, the reflection of the stars a stew in the tumult of the river. How loud it was, in the quiet night. Then Isabella heard something else, too. What was it? She turned her head, trying to catch the sound. As it grew louder, she identified it—the dull concussion of hooves on wet, heavy ground. Horsemen, traveling unusually fast for the time of night.

Isabella hurried off the bridge and pressed against the supports, willing herself to be invisible.

A minute passed. Another. Then all of a sudden, they were there—men on horseback clattering over the bridge and up the hill . . . six . . . eight . . . ten of them. Sweat lathered the necks of the animals. Their iron shoes bit the cobbles, throwing up sparks. The riders were cloaked and booted, hats pressed over their brows. They hurtled on, horses slipping and skittering over the muddy stones.

Isabella's heart contracted; she feared the worst. Priest hunters! Who else would be riding into town at such a pace? Her weariness fell away, and she ran after the riders, following them to Silver Street. Then, keeping to the shadows, she watched the scene unfold.

Horses milled about in front of the Dyers' house. All but

three of the men had dismounted, and their leader banged on the door with his fist. Isabella caught a glimpse of his face. It was Kit Merrivale.

The hammering on the door was loud enough to wake the town. Nearby, a dog began to bark; then another. Isabella was torn. Should she go to the back of the house and try to help the Dyers?

Too late. At a word from Merrivale, three men strode along the alley to block the escape route. He banged again on the door. "Open up," he called out in a low, hoarse voice. "Open up in the name of Her Majesty, Queen Elizabeth. Open the door, or I shall break it down."

All across Maumesbury now, dogs were barking. Isabella sensed the awakening of the nearby townspeople in their homes, the eyes peeping through windows or doors just cracked opened. But no one came into the street. Perhaps they were too afraid, she thought. Or perhaps they were pleased at this raid on the home of their Catholic neighbors.

At last, Elizabeth's mother opened the door. Her face was gray in the light of the candle she held, her hair disarrayed as though she had just climbed out of bed. Isabella was afraid Mistress Dyer would give way to her feelings again, dissolving into tears, but the woman's face was hard as stone.

"What do you want?" she asked, her voice clear and cold.

Merrivale didn't wait for an answer. He pushed Mistress Dyer out of his path and strode into the house. He shouted to the men in the alley, who entered at the back. Others lit torches and trooped inside. The mounted men remained in the street, holding the reins of the horses. The restless little herd twisted and stamped their feet, the steam from their

103

hot bodies and the clouds of their breath swirling about them in the darkness.

Isabella crept nearer. She had to see more. Dodging hooves, she scuttled behind the horses and pressed herself into a doorway, so that she could peer across the narrow street into the Dyers' wide front window.

It was hard to make out exactly what was happening. The house was a dark box where the brilliant red and gold light of the men's torches flared and died away as they walked back and forth through the room. Merrivale stood beside Jane Dyer. Mary cowered at her mistress's side, gripping her shawl like a child.

Isabella could hear the other men calling back and forth. Presumably they were searching the house. And they would find him, of course—the priest, Thomas Montford. Isabella didn't want them to find him—for Elizabeth's sake, and because she liked him, too. She wished for his safety. She prayed for it, for a miracle. But how could he have escaped? There had been so little time between her departure and Merrivale's arrival.

Isabella screwed up her eyes, trying to see what was happening inside. Someone was coming downstairs now. One of the searchers was carrying a child in his arms. It was Elizabeth's little sister, surely, in her white nightgown. Yes, the man was holding Esther, no doubt taken from the warmth of her bed.

The little girl reached for her mother, but the man passed her to Merrivale, who jogged her up and down, a cruel smile on his face. Mistress Dyer's impassive expression faltered. Her mouth moved, but Isabella couldn't hear what she said. The little girl was crying now, her hair spilling from her white cap.

Isabella shivered. Would Merrivale hurt her? The spectacle filled her with cold horror, the man holding the little girl, the mother powerless to stop him. He spoke, and Mistress Dyer shook her head. Esther struggled, her face turned toward her mother, her arms still outstretched. Merrivale wiped the tears from the girl's cheek, but the act wasn't comforting. Mistress Dyer shook her head again and again, but he didn't let the child go.

Isabella clenched her hands together with helpless frustration. *Put her down,* she willed. *Leave them alone.*

The front door swung open, and the men spilled into the street, speaking loudly. They were angry now, the search apparently unsuccessful. Merrivale stepped out, too, beckoning to the men with the horses. One of the riders bent down low, and Merrivale whispered to him. His mount stamped its foot, tossed its head, ground its teeth noisily on its bit. The rider sat up straight and nodded.

Merrivale dropped Esther to the ground. The little girl clutched for her mother, but the men pulled Mistress Dyer away. Still dressed only in her shift and shawl, she was dragged into the street and placed on one of the horses, in front of the rider.

Esther ran after her, shrieking. "Where are you taking my mother? Let her go!" She launched herself at one of the men, waving her arms, trying to kick out, but he simply pushed her over into the muddy street and rolled her out of the way with his foot.

Merrivale and the rest of his men mounted their horses.

They called out to one another; then they all wheeled around and clattered back over the cobbles.

Isabella feared for the small, vulnerable little girl still lying curled up on the icy ground. As soon as the horses were gone, she ran forward.

"Esther!" she whispered. "Did they hurt you?" She tried to pick Esther up, but the little girl resisted, her body tensed into a tight white ball, her sobbing low and indistinct.

"Mary, help me," she called. The servant woman was in the doorway, caught in the same shock as Esther, gazing into space, her mouth opening and closing. "Mary!" Isabella called again. The irritation in her voice seemed to startle the servant from her terrified dream. Mary gasped and crossed herself, then crossed herself again. She started to cry, too, as she hurried out of the house and bent over Esther.

"Come along, little one," she crooned, her voice wavering. "You can't lie out here. We've got to get you inside. We have to clean you up and put you to bed, or your mother will be angry when she comes home again."

This mention of her mother brought another bout of sobbing, but Esther's body softened. Mary picked her up, and Esther curled her arms and legs around the housekeeper. Burdened by the clinging body, Mary could hardly walk, but she managed to carry Esther inside and to the kitchen. Isabella followed.

The house had been turned upside down. The long table and benches were tipped over, the wooden chest emptied, pewter plates strewn across the floor. In the kitchen every pot, bowl, knife, and cup had been thrown onto the flagstones, and flour and dried fruit lay scattered everywhere.

Isabella could hardly breathe. The house stank of the pitchy torches and of the men, their stale breath and the cindery scent of their anger and frustration.

She righted a bench, and Mary sat down, moaning and rocking Esther against herself till the girl fell into an exhausted sleep.

"What am I going to do?" Mary said, over and over. "What am I going to do without the mistress?"

"Where do you think they've taken her?" Isabella said.

The old woman shook her head.

"What happened to the priest? Where did he go?"

At this, Mary gave a low, bitter laugh. "Oh, the priest," she said. She stood up, still cradling Esther. "Come. I'll show you."

They walked through the house, stepping over the wreckage, and went upstairs. Mary laid Esther in her own bed and led Isabella into the large bedroom at the front of the house, where the master and mistress slept. She dropped to her knees by the fireplace, pressing her hands to the bare floorboards near the hearth. Then she ran her fingertips over the nubby surface, reading the grooves and runnels in the wood.

"Here it is," she said. A stab of a finger in a knothole, and a small piece of floorboard was levered out. She put her hand underneath this first piece and lifted away a longer section, revealing, under the floor, the face of the fugitive priest, Thomas Montford.

"They've gone. They've taken the mistress, but you are safe," Mary murmured. And Isabella detected a repressed anger in the woman's voice, that their guest should be free while her mistress had been taken away in the night.

Mary removed another slim plank, exposing the rest of a shallow, coffinlike hiding place. There was barely enough room for the big man—certainly no room to move while the boots of the queen's men tramped just an inch above him. The priest's eyes were full of dirt he had not been able to brush away.

How horrible, Isabella thought, *to be wedged into such a small space, unable to do anything but wait and hope.*

As Thomas struggled out, Mary glanced at Isabella. "It's an old hiding place," she said. "It was made years ago, when the monastery was dissolved. I never thought I'd see the day it would be used again."

Thomas straightened his clothes and wiped his face. He looked from the green girl to the muttering servant woman. "Where's Esther?" he said.

Mary gestured to the door. "I've put her to bed—and Miss Elizabeth is safe at the manor, God be praised. But what about the mistress? What about *her?*" And she moaned again, overcome by the loss, and pressed her apron to her face.

The priest stood up straight, taking charge. He placed his hand on the old woman's sagging shoulder. "Don't lose faith," he said. "I don't believe she's in danger. They can prove nothing against her. She will be questioned, that is all."

This prospect did not seem to reassure Mary, who wept more copiously into her apron.

Thomas turned to Isabella. "I shall leave immediately," he said.

"Where will you go?"

"I was hoping you might be able to help me," he said. "You have lived in the forest. There must be secret places nobody knows about but you. Until I can send a message for help and travel to another safe place, I am in your hands, Isabella."

12

Portrait

When the household had settled down for the night and the cook was fast asleep and snoring, Elizabeth sneaked outside. She hurried across the yard to the stables and curled up in the straw of Isabella's stall, waiting for her friend to return.

The wait seemed to last forever, and Elizabeth spent the time chewing over the events of the evening. She was still racked with indecision. One minute she was furious with herself for confiding in Isabella; the next she was berating herself for putting Isabella in danger, involving her in a life-and-death matter that had nothing whatsoever to do with her. When this conundrum had been exhausted, Elizabeth tormented herself with worries about Isabella's tales of the forest spirits. Was it right for her to trust a girl who consorted with devils? Had she let her judgment be clouded by some kind of sorcery? Then she felt guilty for thinking such terrible things about her friend.

However much she wrestled with the facts, Elizabeth could find no answer. She had nothing safe to cling to, no one to help or advise her, no one to trust. And beneath the constant to-and-fro in her head was the huge and unavoidable concern for the safety of her loved ones—Robert, Esther, and her mother—for Mary and for the priest.

Merrivale hadn't returned to the manor yet. Earlier in the evening, Lady Catherine had anxiously looked for him, delaying the serving of the meal until it was certain he wouldn't be back. She'd been impatient and restless—snapping at Elizabeth, shouting at the servants—and had retired early, complaining of a headache. Elizabeth had helped her undress, untying the stiff corset and skirts. Then she'd brushed Lady Catherine's long hair. But she'd been distracted, and Lady Catherine had been waspish with disappointment, so the comfortable companionship the two usually enjoyed was absent.

Now Elizabeth curled up in the straw. She hoped that Isabella would return soon. Before too long the head groom would check up on the horses, giving them a final supper before turning in. She didn't want him to discover that Isabella was missing.

Elizabeth was warm, lying in the straw wrapped up in Isabella's blanket. Eventually, she dozed, weary of thinking and worrying. She dreamed of the green girl dancing in a circle with creatures that possessed the bodies of men and the legs and feet of birds. The spectacle filled her with horror, and when the dream Isabella beckoned her to join in the ugly, disjointed dance, Elizabeth cried out. But a cold hand pressed over her mouth.

Elizabeth's eyes flicked open. It was very dark, but dimly she made out a mossy face and a swag of hair. Isabella!

The green girl was hot and out of breath. She raised a finger to her lips and then withdrew her other hand from Elizabeth's face. The stable door rattled. In an instant Isabella had drawn the blanket over Elizabeth and partly across her own body. She slipped her wrist back into the iron manacle.

Elizabeth couldn't see anything, but she heard the clank of a wooden pail on the flagstones and smelled the tallow from a lantern. The horses moved about restlessly, anticipating their supper. A man spoke in a low voice to them, moving from one to another. He paused a moment by Isabella's stall, then moved on. Isabella squeezed Elizabeth's arm. It seemed he hadn't noticed anything amiss. At last, the stable door opened and shut again, and everything was quiet, except for the sound of the horses chewing their meal.

Isabella threw back the blanket, and the girls sat up. Elizabeth waited for her friend to speak, but the green girl hesitated.

"What happened?" Elizabeth asked anxiously. "Did you see my family? Did you warn them—and the priest?"

"Elizabeth," Isabella whispered, "I will tell you. Just be patient—listen to me." She took Elizabeth's hand in her own, but Elizabeth pulled it away. She didn't want comfort now; she wanted to know.

"What is it?" she demanded. "Tell me!"

Isabella swallowed. "They came in the night, Elizabeth. Merrivale and his men on horseback. They went to your house and searched it. They took your mother."

Elizabeth stared. Then she began to suck in quick, deep breaths, thoughts racing unbidden through her head. How could this have happened? Hadn't they prayed for God's help? Weren't they faithful enough? She pictured her mother dragged into the street. Where would they take her? What would they do? Terrible images arose. The authorities were cruel, and the punishments meted out even to petty criminals were swift and savage. She began to shake. She tried to speak, but the words wouldn't come out.

"Elizabeth, Elizabeth," Isabella said urgently. "It might not be as bad as you think." She lowered her voice. "They didn't take the priest—they couldn't find him because he was hidden under the floorboards. He said they would question your mother, but they have no evidence against her."

Elizabeth turned numbly to Isabella, trying to absorb her words. "Esther?" she said. There were no rules exempting children from questioning—or even torture. "Esther and Mary?"

"They're together at home," Isabella reassured her. "They're safe—at least for the time being."

Elizabeth nodded. But her mother . . . what about her mother? And Robert. Had he been taken from the university? There was no way of knowing.

Isabella pushed the hair from Elizabeth's face and embraced her, offering comfort. Elizabeth blinked and sniffed. She pulled back and looked at the green girl. "Why are you so kind to me?" she asked. "You've risked your life by helping me. Why should you do that?"

"You're the first friend I've ever had, Elizabeth. I *want* to help you," Isabella said simply.

Elizabeth shook her head, trying to get the better of her feelings, to think straight. "Where is the priest?" she asked. "Is he also safe?"

She sensed, rather than saw, a smile on Isabella's face.

"For the moment, yes," Isabella said. "That's why it took me so long to return. I led him to the shrine by the spring, where you found me. He seemed glad to be there. He is a kind and brave man, Elizabeth. I wanted to help him, too."

Elizabeth nodded. The shrine was not a place Merrivale and his men would find in the night, but it wouldn't be safe for long. In the daytime, the local people foraged for firewood there and drove their pigs among the trees to feed on nuts and roots.

"It was a good choice," she said. "But tomorrow he'll have to move again. We must find another safe house."

The two girls talked a bit more, but Elizabeth didn't dare stay long. She embraced Isabella, bade her goodnight, and ran back to the house. To her relief, the cook was still snoring when she climbed beneath the blanket.

Elizabeth's mind was awhirl as she thought about her mother's plight and the task ahead, considered the options, and made plans. But finally she fell so deeply asleep that she didn't hear the cook arise, the usual morning noises in the kitchen didn't disturb her, and she didn't wake up until the chamberlain himself came to rouse her.

"Lady Catherine wants you," he said abruptly, and Elizabeth struggled out of bed. She dressed quickly and arranged her hair, still tucking the stray locks into her cap as she hurried up the stairs and along the corridor. All the servants stared as she passed. No one said a word.

They know, Elizabeth realized with dread. *They know!* She tapped on the chamber door, then entered, willing herself not to show her fear.

Lady Catherine was standing at the window, already

dressed. She motioned Elizabeth to the window seat. Then she clasped her hands nervously and gazed outside. "Elizabeth, I have some bad news for you," she said. "Your mother was arrested last night on suspicion of harboring a fugitive priest. She is being held for questioning." She gave Elizabeth a quick glance, as if expecting tears or an emotional outburst. But Elizabeth remained still and cold.

"How do you know this?" Elizabeth asked, trying to keep her voice level.

"Kit supervised the arrest," Lady Catherine said, once again staring out the window. "He told me when he returned this morning. Of course, this makes things difficult for me. It might not be wise to have a girl from a suspect Catholic family in my household, now that an arrest has been made."

Elizabeth pressed her lips together, remaining silent. Did Lady Catherine mean to dismiss her?

But Lady Catherine was not as chilly as her words suggested. She sat down beside Elizabeth and grasped her shoulder tightly. "We've been friends, haven't we, Elizabeth?" she said. "All the long days you brightened for me when I was on my own . . . I haven't forgotten them."

Elizabeth nodded. It was true. For two years now she had come—sometimes several days a week—to listen to Lady Catherine, help with her painting, read Greek and Latin, act as a confidante for her grumbles about life in the country and as an audience for her tales about life at court.

Lady Catherine drew a breath. "Would you do something for me, Elizabeth?"

"Of course," Elizabeth said. "What is it you want?"

"Would you convert to the Protestant faith?"

"What?" Elizabeth said in shock. She couldn't believe it. Was Lady Catherine serious? Convert to the Church of England? Abandon her family and faith to save her own skin? Never. *Never!* Her thoughts tumbled over one another. If she said no, would Lady Catherine withdraw her protection and hand Elizabeth over to Merrivale? Then what? How would saying no help her family—and the priest?

"Would you convert to the Protestant faith?" Lady Catherine repeated. "Would you stay with me here at the manor and be safe? Be a daughter to me? I am so very fond of you."

"Lady Catherine, I—I don't know what to say." Elizabeth stumbled over the words, struggling to find a way out.

Lady Catherine gave her a long, searching look. "I appreciate that this is a difficult decision and that you will need time to think and pray," she said. "We will speak of this again soon."

Elizabeth knew her mistress was a clever woman. Her unusual occupation and dazzling success as a woman artist at the court had required huge reserves of cunning, tact, and diplomacy. She had to know when to speak and when to be quiet. When it was sensible to flatter and when it was better to be honest. Had she come under pressure from Kit to hand over her lady in waiting? Was Lady Catherine using this invitation to think about conversion to protect Elizabeth and give her a bit of time to make plans?

Elizabeth stood and bobbed a little curtsey. "Thank you. Yes, I will think on it," she said gratefully.

Lady Catherine nodded. "I have no sympathy with heretic priests who come here to stir up trouble," she said.

"But I am sorry for you that your mother has been taken. I pray she will soon be released."

Lady Catherine breakfasted on porridge and honey, but Elizabeth was quite unable to eat, dreading the moment she would have to face Kit Merrivale again. That moment came sooner than she expected.

"Kit wants his portrait painted," Lady Catherine said, as if in warning. "Keep up your courage, Elizabeth. I shall need your assistance." She pushed aside her breakfast dishes and led the way downstairs.

Lady Catherine worked in a long, low-ceilinged room on the first floor, with windows to the south and west that filled the space with light. Stepping into the room, Elizabeth breathed in the familiar perfume of linseed oil, the base for the rich paints. The place was cluttered with canvases, some half covered with unfinished paintings, some newly stretched and primed. She helped Lady Catherine select a suitable canvas and set it up on an easel. Then she set to work grinding pigments to make up fresh paint for the portrait.

The previous summer Elizabeth had spent many happy hours with Lady Catherine, mixing paints, talking to her while she worked. It had been a soothing and intriguing distraction from the drudgery and straitened circumstances at home. Then Lady Catherine had grown bored and lonely, and her painting had fallen by the wayside. The room had been shut up. It was strange and unsettling for Elizabeth to return now, as if her present fears were polluting the good memories locked inside.

Using a stone mortar and pestle, Elizabeth ground the pigments: ochre for yellow and brown, cinnabar for red, and precious lapis lazuli for blue. The work was tricky and absorbing. She did not look up when Kit walked in, dressed in his white shirt and wide leather breeches. But peeking through her lashes, she quietly observed Lady Catherine stretch out her hands to his in greeting; observed, too, the smile on her face, the fluttering and flirting that followed.

It was all very well to be clever, thought Elizabeth, but cleverness was obviously no protection for a lonely woman long deprived of attention and admiration. Lady Catherine might understand what kind of man Kit was, and she certainly knew he was responsible for arrests and nighttime raids. She was prepared to scheme against him for the protection of her lady in waiting, but still she blushed when he stepped into the room, and she smiled too much and laughed a curious giddy laugh. What was it about him that attracted her? His pretty face, perhaps? His careless air and fancy clothes? His aura of confidence and power?

Elizabeth lifted her gaze from her work and looked at Kit, trying to be objective. Why *shouldn't* Lady Catherine like him? He was handsome and respected, and he worked for the protection of the realm. But Elizabeth was still angry with Lady Catherine for being susceptible. Her mistress was making a fool of herself. After all, she was older than Kit, and even though she hadn't seen her husband for months, she was still married.

Elizabeth listened to Merrivale charm and flirt and at the same time imagined him breaking into her home, seizing her mother and locking her up in a cold cell, bullying, threatening, taking full advantage of his strength and power. She banged the mortar fiercely into the pigment, feeling for him a profound hatred. She knew that Jesus said to love your enemies, to pray for those who persecuted you. But she could not pray for Christopher Merrivale—except to pray he might one day find himself cold, alone, and friendless in a pit full of rats, awaiting the kind of fate he now meted out to Catholic priests and helpless women.

As if sensing the feelings burning inside her, Merrivale turned to look at her. "I think your lady in waiting wishes she were grinding my skull in her bowl," he observed. "A fine ivory color it would make, wouldn't it?"

Lady Catherine smiled briefly. "Come," she said. "Sit here by the window, so I have the sunlight upon you."

She placed him at a desk, with a book in his hand and a dagger visible at his belt. On the desk she arranged a flower, a candle, and a skull—symbols of mortality. She fussed over his position, sideways to the painter with his upper body turned toward her, so that in the portrait he would face the viewer. It was a long process, and an hour had passed before Lady Catherine was satisfied. She settled his clothing neatly, brushed the hair from his face, moved his elbow forward and back again, seeking a perfect compositional balance. During this time, Elizabeth observed, Lady Catherine was indifferent to Merrivale as a man. She was absorbed in the process of her work. Finally, she stepped back to the canvas and swiftly made a deft sketch.

"My men will continue questioning the woman today," Merrivale said lazily. He addressed Lady Catherine, but Elizabeth knew the statement was made for her benefit. She tried to make no response.

"We know well enough the priest was at the house. It is

only a matter of time before we find him. I'm certain she will tell us where he is."

Elizabeth turned away, but not before a gasp escaped her lips. Had Merrivale noticed?

Lady Catherine didn't encourage him in this line of conversation. Instead, she made a comment about the portrait.

Merrivale ignored her. "Do you know where the priest is, Elizabeth?" he said.

Lady Catherine broke in. "Of course she doesn't! She's been here with me! Leave her alone, Kit. Isn't it bad enough for the poor girl to know that her mother has been arrested?"

Merrivale fixed his gaze on Lady Catherine. "You are not sympathetic to the Catholics, are you?" he said, teasing.

"No, I'm not," she responded angrily. "But Elizabeth isn't a heretic. She's loyal to me. Please let her be."

"Then she's your responsibility, Catherine. I don't want her leaving the house or speaking to any of her family members. No letters, Elizabeth. Do you understand?"

Elizabeth nodded.

Merrivale looked at her again, cold and assessing. He said no more about the priest. But when at last they left the room for their midday meal, he reached out to grasp a blond curl that had escaped from Elizabeth's cap. Without a word he gave it a tug, hard enough to hurt.

Elizabeth stared at him. She knew what Merrivale was thinking. If he didn't get what he wanted, she would be next on his list, and Lady Catherine would not be able to protect her. *Be afraid, little girl,* he said without words. And Elizabeth was afraid.

13

Shelter

The kitchen was full of steam sent up by buckets of hot water poured into a wooden tub set in front of the fire. The men had been driven out, as had the dogs, leaving Lady Catherine, her dress covered in a white pinafore, presiding over a herd of female servants. A large brick of cream-colored soap waited on the table—along with a sharp knife.

Isabella hovered at the edge of the room, knowing what the preparations presaged. She dreaded the inevitable scrubbing and, more than that, the humiliation of being stripped and handled by these women, who seemed to believe that they were being kind. *Ah, well,* she thought glumly, *perhaps if I look more like them, I will be accepted. Perhaps people won't be frightened of me anymore.*

Finally, the preparations were complete. Lady Catherine turned to Isabella. "Take off your clothes," she said briskly. "Come now, Isabella. It won't be so bad. I take a full bath at least twice a year, and it does me no harm at all."

Everyone stared at Isabella, and she shivered to be the center of so much attention. But what choice did she have?

Retaining as much dignity as possible, she slipped off her old tunic and stepped into the tub. She had never bathed like this before, and the slide of clear, warm water upon her bare skin felt strange. Did she like the sensation? There was no chance to think about it. The women descended, armed with pieces of cloth and soap, and she was unceremoniously scrubbed, rubbed, dunked, and rinsed. Caught up in the storm of enthusiastic washing, Isabella surrendered. Her eyes and ears were soon full of soap, her skin raw from the women's endeavors to get through the green to her natural color. Then her nails were trimmed with a paring knife, and her long rug of matted hair was cut short.

Isabella felt a pang to lose it. It had served as a cloak, a blanket, a form of protection. Now it lay on the wet flagstones like a soggy animal pelt. At last, she was dried off with a blanket and presented with a linen shift, a long woolen dress, and a pair of plain leather shoes to wear. Lady Catherine tugged a white woolen cap on her head, tucking the shorn ends of her hair under the hem. Then the women all stood back to make an assessment of their work. There were murmurs of satisfaction and self-congratulation. Lady Catherine smiled.

"A great improvement," she said. "At least you resemble a Christian now."

Isabella gave a wry smile, trying to look grateful. Despite the covering of clothes, she felt bare without her hair. She shook her head, unused to its lightness. The dress was scratchy and constricting, and her feet felt trapped and awkward in the shoes. She peered at the backs of her hands. The skin was still green, but the color had faded a little. And how did she feel about this? Isabella tested her emotions and found them ambivalent. She wanted to be human again, to live among her own people. At the same time, she was not entirely comfortable with her transformation—it was as though the well-meaning women had washed away some of her very being along with the green stain. Still, she mustered a smile and made a clumsy attempt at a curtsey, which prompted a ripple of applause from the gathering.

Now suitably clean and dressed, Isabella was allowed to stay in the house. Lady Catherine gave her a tour as if intrigued by a new toy, the girl from the woods. If she expected Isabella to marvel, she must have been disappointed, because Isabella didn't say very much. When they stepped into the room where Lady Catherine painted, Isabella spotted Elizabeth cleaning brushes. She nodded a greeting when Lady Catherine introduced them, but she was careful to keep her face neutral.

At nightfall, a rainstorm drove in from the west, and the household was grateful to remain sheltered inside. Isabella was given chores in the kitchen . . . chopping turnips, popping beans from their pods. She felt uneasy among so many people. She wasn't used to company. She stared out the window and thought of the priest alone in the leaky hermitage in the woods. He would be hungry after a day without food. Doubtless, despite his courage, fears would be gnawing at him, too. She had to find a way to talk with Elizabeth, to make a plan to see the priest and find him somewhere safer to stay.

When the household gathered for the meal that night, Isabella was the center of attention, the marvelous wild girl brought in from the forest. Everyone wanted to pinch her skin or see her teeth or talk to her. They asked questions she refused to answer and jested that she might have a tail or claws on her feet. They wanted to know how she had lived in the forest and why she was green.

Isabella wouldn't speak to anyone, and as the night wore on and the beer took effect, the questions became louder and more intrusive. Isabella suffered in the welter of people, the babble of voices, and the scent of unwashed, overheated bodies and rich, spicy food. She was conscious of Elizabeth, similarly isolated in the crowd, and of Kit Merrivale, who talked and drank with the lord's men yet kept himself aloof and observant, never letting down his guard. Isabella suspected he considered himself better than they, for his eyes were ever chilly and disdainful.

At last, Lady Catherine took pity on Isabella, bidding the servants to leave her alone. She asked Elizabeth to escort the girl to a straw mattress she'd had set up in the hall close to her own bedroom. "You are about the same age as Isabella," she said. "Perhaps you could be friends. Take care of her, Elizabeth. See if you can draw her out."

Isabella suppressed a smile. How fortunate was this turn of events!

Elizabeth bobbed a curtsey, took up a candle, and gestured for Isabella to follow her. Once outside the dining hall, she linked arms with Isabella. "Let's go to Lady Catherine's workroom," she whispered. "We shall have privacy there."

The room was cold and quiet. On the easel, the painting of Kit Merrivale waited. Three colors blocked in the background, Merrivale's body, and the pale oval of his face. Elizabeth scowled at it as she passed by.

The two girls sat down together. "You look so different," Elizabeth marveled. "I hardly recognized you at first." A few locks of hair had escaped from Isabella's cap. Elizabeth stretched out a hand to touch the blunt ends. "Was it terrible when they did this to you?"

Isabella shook her head. "Not really," she said. "And at least I don't look like a devil anymore."

"No, you look more . . . ordinary," Elizabeth said a little regretfully. She looked down for a moment; then she went on. "I'm ashamed to tell you this, but I did wonder at first if you might be in league with the devil. But I know now it can't be so. I think you're an angel, Isabella."

Isabella shook her head with a snort. "Don't be silly," she said.

Elizabeth regarded her with surprise.

"I'm not an angel, and we haven't time for this," Isabella said crossly. "What are we going to do about the priest? Where should we take him?"

Elizabeth blinked at this sudden change in the conversation. "I've put some food aside for him," she said. "When I took a meal to Lady Catherine and Merrivale at midday, I told the cook they needed extra because they were so hungry." She looked away, wrinkling her forehead. "It's odd how easy it is to lie when you know the person you're lying to hates you."

Isabella gazed at her friend. Elizabeth looked tired and pale. "They hate the idea of you being a Catholic," she said. "They don't really hate *you*. Try not to take it to heart."

Elizabeth looked puzzled. "How would you know?"

Isabella smiled sadly. "I've been listening to the servants

talk. And my mother said exactly the same thing to me, when people took against us."

"What happened to your mother?" Elizabeth said. "And what about your brother?"

"I don't want to talk about my mother. But John? You can help me find him."

Elizabeth nodded. "I will do everything I can," she said.

"Thank you. But first we have to think about the priest and your mother," said Isabella. "What do you want me to do?"

Elizabeth took a deep breath. "My family was entrusted with a secret by the monks of the old abbey," she said. "This is the most precious of secrets—and not to be divulged. But it might be of service now."

Isabella nodded. She sensed how much it cost Elizabeth to speak of it.

"You must tell the priest to wait for me in the old chapel," Elizabeth said. "It is the only part of the abbey that King Henry did not destroy. The people use it as their parish church now, for . . . for the Church of England."

Swiftly, Elizabeth explained what the priest must do and the nature of her family's secret. "I swore to my father I would tell no one except my own children," Elizabeth concluded bitterly. "Now I have betrayed my father's trust—and his father's and grandfather's. But what else can I do?"

Isabella squeezed her friend's arm. "I think your father would have done the same," she whispered. "Have faith."

They agreed it would be safer for Isabella to make the journey again: she traveled faster than Elizabeth could and knew the woods better. And if she was caught out of the house, she might be scolded or punished, but in the same circumstances Elizabeth would certainly be arrested. So, when the household had finally settled down for the night and Lady Catherine had retired to bed, Isabella took off her punishing shoes and tied up her skirt. Then, taking the food Elizabeth had provided, she set off through the rainy night to the forest and the hidden priest.

Despite the hurly-burly of the wind and weather, Isabella was relieved to be outside and on her own again. The storm was exhilarating. She could see in the dark as well as a fox, and she passed over the mud with swift, light feet. The forest embraced her like a long-lost friend; the trees offered comforting shelter, a place where she felt at home.

"Thomas? Thomas Montford?" she called out when she reached the broken hut by the shrine. Peering into the murky shelter, she spotted the priest crouched at the back, trying to avoid the worst of the leaks in the roof.

"Isabella? Is that you?" The priest unfolded, rising to his feet. "I thought you were a wolf. You move like a wild animal." The previous night she had guided him through the forest, holding his hand. He had been noisy and clumsy beside her, walking into branches, tripping over brambles.

"I brought you food and candles," Isabella said. "Elizabeth stole them from the manor. She asked me to beg your forgiveness for the sin, but she couldn't let you go hungry."

Thomas laughed. "Of course she is forgiven. Didn't Our Lord tell us to feed the hungry?" He was ravenous and tucked into the bread and cheese and cold vegetable stew as though he hadn't eaten for a week. When he had finished, he wiped his mouth with the back of his hand and sighed.

"Now," he said. "I know of safe houses in York, but it is a long way off, and I don't have a horse. How I am to get there?"

"What about those you'd leave behind?" Isabella asked. "What about Elizabeth's mother?"

"She doesn't know where I am. Even if she confesses I was in the house, they won't find me there. Don't worry about that."

Isabella frowned. The priest's answer was chilling. Didn't he care what happened to the woman who had sheltered him? Was his own safety his only concern? "I didn't mean that. I want to know how we can get her released," Isabella said coldly.

The priest was taken aback. "You think me uncaring?" he said. "I am sworn to restore the true faith, Isabella. I would give up my life like that"—he snapped his fingers—"if it were needed. Yet I don't disdain life. No, indeed, I love it. It is here the sun shines, and I'm greedy for it. But what does it profit a man if he gain the whole world but loses his own soul? Jane's fate lies in God's hands, not in mine."

Isabella was not convinced. She had suffered too much under the weight of people's convictions. She would help him all the same, for Elizabeth's sake, and for Jane Dyer's. But she understood the fever of faith in Thomas Montford and knew that he would have her burned if he learned of her relationship with the crow people. He would accuse her of witchcraft, as the townsfolk had accused her mother, and think he was saving her soul as he consigned her to the flames. A heavy sadness settled on her heart. She had hidden for three hundred years, and nothing had changed.

There was a moment of silence between them. "Light the

candle," she said at last. "I have something to show you."

Thomas did as she'd asked. The flame flickered, and in the wavering light, Isabella found the loose brick in the chimney that Elizabeth had found just a few days before.

"Elizabeth told me to show you this," she said to the priest. "She said the walls of the abbey were torn down, but the abbey was much more than stones and mortar. The abbey was a great center for learning, and although much was destroyed, some of the books and parchments survived, hidden away in secret places—like this one." She pushed her hand into the space behind the brick and pulled out the sooty roll of parchment.

The priest looked from Isabella to the parchment. Excitement colored his face. He nodded.

"Elizabeth knows another one of these secret places, and she will show you where it is. She will meet you in the chapel in the old abbey, if she can get away from the manor. Wait there tomorrow in the middle of the day."

"In the abbey chapel? I might be noticed. What if people ask who I am?"

"You have to take the risk," Isabella said. "If someone asks, make something up. Say that you're a traveling merchant, that you have business in the town."

The priest stared at the thick, grimy papers rolled up in his hand. "God bless you, Isabella," he said.

14

The Baby

sabella ran through the rain, her skirts catching on branches and brambles. Her legs were plastered with cold clinging mud. Twigs swiped at her face. She was clumsy, not concentrating on the journey, her thoughts knotted.

She didn't want to remember the past. Living with the crow people, she'd found it easy to avoid thinking about that terrible time. But thorns were still lodged in her heart, and now the priest's words had set the wounds stinging.

The day the baby boy had been born to the Watts family was the day Isabella had seen a faerie for the first time. She saw more after that, around the cottage she shared with her mother and brother, in the woods and fields. Not fully visible, not entirely in the earthly world, but there nonetheless. She realized that she had lived in the presence of the crow people all her life—without ever knowing it. But the ceremony by the spring had revealed them to her. She could sense them often now, would catch a glimpse out of the corner of her eye, feel a prickling of the skin on the back of her arms, come upon a thread of enticing, otherworldly perfume. The faerie world, the shadow land, was close at hand.

The baking, golden summer passed away, the nights closed in, and the forest green fell in tatters of gold and scarlet. Men herded their pigs into the woods to feed on fallen acorns.

For weeks after the birth of the infant, the Leland family was well provided for. The first gift to appear was a bolt of blue cloth, which Ruth made into a new dress for Isabella, who was growing fast. Then food was left by the garden gate: grapes from the abbey vineyards, sweet apples, tasty fruitcakes, and nuts. Isabella was delighted by the gifts, and Ruth made every effort to look pleased. But Isabella sensed her unease, and for the first time she noticed the deepening signs of age in her mother's face—fine lines around her mouth and a deeper line across the bridge of her nose.

"What's wrong?" she would ask when her mother sighed, but Ruth only replied with a smile and a dismissive shake of her head. The teaching went on as before, except that Ruth seemed more eager than ever to impart her store of knowledge, reminding her daughter of previous lessons, testing her, allowing her to take over the preparation of medicines for the people who came to the gate with their endless procession of ailments. And without any help from her mother, Isabella developed her knowledge of the crow people.

When bowls moved on the table or bundles of herbs dropped to the floor, Isabella knew the faeries were close at hand. She wasn't afraid of them. She strained her eyes to see, hungry to know them better. She remembered the godlike creature her mother had summoned at the spring. Sometimes he stole into her dreams—always far away, always out of reach. And once, in the depths of the night, she woke to hear the beating of huge wings over the cottage and imagined the faerie—black and gold, dressed in his crow feathers— planting his thin, long-nailed feet upon the ridge of the thatched roof.

In the half-light at evening and dawn, the view of the forest from the rear window of the house sometimes became something else—mountains sheltering a stone palace whose windows were ablaze with firelight, or a glade where a faerie girl ran, her long hair floating over matte white skin.

Ruth did not comment or explain these happenings. She sat nursing baby John or embroidering white daisies on the hem of Isabella's new blue dress, as if life were going on as usual. But in spirit, she was far away. Isabella sensed the distance growing between them, and for the first time she felt lonely.

Autumn darkened into winter. After the unseasonably hot summer, the winter retaliated with weeks of ice and snow. Even the river around Maumesbury froze. There was nothing to do on the long dark nights but stoke the fire and huddle close to the hearth. Ruth recounted again the tales of the kings and queens of the shadow land, the adventures of faerie knights, their loves and conquests.

On Ash Wednesday, snow gave way to rain, and the river broke out of its skin of ice, flooding the neighboring fields. There was mud everywhere, and an icy driving wind. The animals cowered, shivering and forlorn, in makeshift shelters, and the people were miserable, too, cursing the weather, the cold and damp that seemed to bide forever.

Then, just before Easter, the sun broke through at last. Eager leaves seemed to cover the bare limbs of the trees in a single night. And a rider came from the house of Mistress Watts, asking Ruth to attend the baby, who was seriously ill.

A shadow crossed Ruth's face when she heard the news. She dropped her head, staring at the ground. She seemed very small now, her shoulders bony from the long winter, the hungry spring.

"Will you come?" the man asked. The tone of his voice did not suggest Ruth had a choice.

She raised her face and nodded. "Ride ahead," she said. "Tell them I'll attend the boy this afternoon. I need to prepare."

The man headed back to the town. Isabella watched the horse pick its way through the mire of the road. She didn't want to look at her mother, who was still standing exactly where the man had left her.

"You're afraid he'll die," Isabella blurted out.

Ruth nodded. "His heart isn't right. I'm surprised he has lived this long."

"Why are you so afraid? Many babies die."

"Yes," Ruth said. "But this time is different. Mistress Watts—she won't accept it."

Isabella chewed her lip. "Perhaps he won't die," she said. "You're an excellent healer. Maybe you can save him."

"Maybe," Ruth said.

Isabella insisted on accompanying her mother to Maumesbury, even though Ruth suggested she stay behind with John. He was toddling now, and his wisps of baby hair were giving way to thick dark curls, but Ruth hoisted him onto her back for the walk to the town.

They were let in the back door by the same dour servant who had questioned Isabella about John's father. Mistress Watts was sitting in the front room of the house, a generous fire roaring in the hearth despite the arrival of warmer weather. The baby lay in a carved wooden cradle beside her. Servants fussed about the room, whispering.

Ruth handed John to Isabella and dipped a little curtsey to the lady of the house. Mistress Watts had changed a great deal over the months. Her fleshy body had not thinned down. Instead, her figure seemed to have sagged. Her face was pouchy now, and gray under the eyes, as though she hadn't been sleeping, and she had a rash of angry spots on her chin.

Ruth stretched out a hand and touched Mistress Watts on the shoulder. "I'm sorry he's ill," she said.

Mistress Watts sighed deeply. She smiled briefly, as though Ruth's presence were enough to soothe her. Then she turned her attention to her child, and other feelings washed over her face: grief, frustration, despair.

"Peter doesn't thrive," she said quietly. "He's nearly ten months old now, and he can't even sit up. I need your help." She looked at Ruth, and her eyes flared, issuing a challenge.

Ruth nodded. "Of course." She picked up the baby from the cradle and loosened the blankets wrapped around him.

Isabella drew a breath. How pale he looked—no, worse than pale. His lips, his skin, were bluish, starved of blood. And how puny, for a ten-month-old child. His limbs were thin and undernourished, and his head flopped. He looked like a rag doll.

Peter stirred as Ruth examined him, and his legs gave a feeble kick. Then he whimpered, his baby face crumpling into an expression of woe. But it seemed too much for him, all too much, as though he didn't have enough strength to share exactly what he felt. The whimper died on his lips.

Ruth ran her hands expertly over the child, feeling his chest, his hands and fingers. She pressed her ear to his ribs, to hear the heart. Everyone stared—the mother, the servants, Isabella, holding her own sturdy baby brother. Ruth's face was warm with compassion for the sick baby, and he calmed beneath her touch. Then she wrapped him up again and held him gently in her arms. "How does he feed?" she asked.

"A struggle, always," Mistress Watts replied. "I have plenty of milk for him, but he doesn't have the strength to suck for long. I have to wake him up to nurse him, otherwise he would just sleep forever. He doesn't even cry." A fat tear welled in her eye and plopped onto her cheek.

A gust of wind puffed a curl of black smoke into the room from the chimney, and the dim chamber was clouded. One of the servants stepped forward and fanned the gritty wood smoke from the baby's face.

"His father despairs of him," Mistress Watts continued. "Thinks he should die instead of lingering. But we waited so long for this child. So long. I couldn't bear to lose him. I don't think there'll be another." A second fat tear dropped onto her cheek, and she wiped it away with the back of her hand. "You can save him, Mistress Leland. I know you can."

She had placed all her hopes on Ruth, and Isabella quailed at the thought of this weight resting on her mother's shoulders.

Ruth handed Peter to his mother. "It's his heart," she said. "It isn't working properly. Put your ear to his chest, and you will hear for yourself how weakly and oddly it beats. There is little that I can do."

The servants muttered indignantly, and Mistress Watts's lips trembled.

"You *can*. You *can* do something," she said. "I understand . . . I have been told . . . that you can work magic. Do what you have to do. Anything—as long as Peter lives."

"I've brought herbs for him," Ruth said, drawing a pouch from her pocket. "Brew them with boiled water, cool the tonic, and feed him drops from a spoon. This will stimulate the heart." She sighed. "Have you consulted the doctors at the abbey? They are skilled men. They would give you another opinion."

"They say his heart is weak, and that he will die. They have washed their hands of him," Mistress Watts said angrily. "But you're different. You can resort to other powers." She turned pleading eyes on Ruth. "I would reward you . . . give you whatever you wanted. Can you do something? Some magic? A charm?"

Ruth shook her head. "What you're asking is beyond me," she said. "There is nothing more I can do."

Mistress Watts's face clouded. "What I don't understand," she said bitterly, "is how my son came to have a heart that doesn't work. How did this happen to him? Why was he born this way?" The words hung like a threat in the smoky room, and the questions had no answer.

At the end of summer, as reapers cut the first wheat in the fields, Death made the small harvest of baby Peter, just two months past his first birthday. Isabella was surprised he had lasted that long. Ruth had seen the baby twice more, but the tonics she prepared had simply delayed the inevitable.

The whole town seemed weighted down by the grief of the Watts family. The lavish funeral was conducted by the abbot, William of Cullerne, but Ruth was not invited to attend.

Mistress Watts would not be consoled. One day she rode out to Ruth's cottage and screamed abuse. She accused Ruth of cursing the baby at birth, of working witchcraft and consorting with demons. She wound herself into a passion, shouting about changelings and stealers of souls.

Isabella peeped out the window, watching the bereaved woman rage. She could feel Mistress Watts's anger break over the cottage like a storm.

"Shall we go out and speak with her?" she asked her mother.

Ruth shook her head, her face drained and pale. "It would do no good. There is nothing I could say to change her mind. She has to blame someone."

Isabella began to shake. "Shall we leave? Shall we run away? We could go into the forest and never come back."

"That would be taken as an admission of guilt," Ruth said. "They would ride after us . . . hunt us down. And how fast could we move with John to carry? Besides, our family has lived here for hundreds of years. Maybe longer. We have always cared for the shrine. This is our place, Isabella. Your place."

Behind them, John began to cry, as though Mistress Watts's rage disturbed him, too. Isabella knelt and embraced him. His eyes were a warm brown curiously flecked with gold. His skin was soft and perfect, like a flower petal, and radiant with health. Isabella's heart swelled with love for him. What wouldn't she do to prevent something bad from happening to him? How would she feel if—like baby Peter—John were snatched away by Death? Her blood ran cold to think of it.

Outside, the demented woman continued to shout and rant till her voice was hoarse. She used terrible words, foul language, the most bitter of curses, calling down the wrath of God upon the heretic, the witch, the paramour of devils. The Lelands cowered in their house, trying in vain not to listen, until evening fell and Master Watts galloped out in search of his wife and finally took her away. As they departed, he looked back at the cottage and spat on the ground.

No one called on Ruth Leland again to seek help for sickness or childbirth. No one came near the cottage. It was as though Mistress Watts's angry voice had settled over the place in a venomous cloud. And if Isabella was out walking and passed some of the local people, they turned away from her and made the sign against evil, balling up a fist, poking a thumb through the fingers.

The tide had turned against the Lelands.

Running through the night, returning to the manor at Spirit Hill, Isabella was swallowed up in the remembering. All this had happened more than three hundred years before, but the images of the last days in her mother's cottage were bright and vivid in her mind; the feelings were fresh and raw. Now the emotions of that terrible time washed through her—the isolation, the constant gnawing fear. Her mother had been the one permanent, essential part of her life—the root of everything, the sunshine, the source of all comfort and protection. But her mother was gone. The world was endlessly hostile, and she was a lost child, alone and helpless, at the mercy of others.

The crow people had taken her in, but they didn't care for her any more than humans might care for birds they threw crumbs to, finding them pleasing one moment but forgetting them the next. The hermit Jerome had befriended her, but he was dead and gone. Now she had Lady Catherine and Elizabeth. Lady Catherine was kind, but it was to Elizabeth that Isabella had given her heart. So much about Elizabeth's life echoed Isabella's—the loneliness, the persecution, the mother and brother in peril. Isabella hadn't been able to save her own mother. But perhaps she could help Elizabeth save hers.

The manor crouched in darkness. Isabella stole into the silent house without waking a soul. The dogs didn't bark at her, wagging their tails instead as she slipped past. But there was no way to disguise the fact that she had been out and about in the night. She was covered in mud, head to foot. Quickly she peeled off the sodden, filthy gown and lay down on the little mattress in the corridor. She would be told off, certainly—perhaps even punished. But no one save Elizabeth would have an idea of what she had been up to.

15

The Deacon

In the morning Elizabeth sat in the kitchen with a bowl of scalding hot porridge before her. The house was relatively quiet, the men and dogs out on some hunting expedition now that the rain had stopped. So when Lady Catherine's voice came from the upstairs corridor, she could hear it clearly. The lady was scolding Isabella for going out during the night, for the filth on her clothes and body. It was a terrible telling-off, ending with the threat of a whipping. But Elizabeth knew the expedition had been a success, because Isabella nodded and gave her a secret smile when she entered the kitchen just minutes later. And then Elizabeth smiled, too.

After breakfast Lady Catherine continued to work on her portrait of Kit Merrivale. Elizabeth attended her, and when her mistress paused a moment, she asked if she could return to Maumesbury to see her little sister, Esther, and to consult with the parish priest about converting to the Church of England. She kept her voice level, looking directly at her mistress, speaking without hesitation.

Lady Catherine turned to Merrivale, in his pose at the

desk. "I have no objections," she said. "What do you say, Kit?"

Merrivale turned his cold eyes on Elizabeth and looked her up and down as if making some kind of calculation. Elizabeth stared straight back. Her dislike of the man had hardened into a kind of courage. She remembered what Thomas had said about putting her fears behind her. She understood him now. Fear would be useless. It would just keep her from doing what had to be done. *Say yes*, she willed. *Say yes, Kit Merrivale.*

"Yes," he said. "Who am *I* to stand in the way of a conversion? But she must be accompanied, of course."

"Certainly," Lady Catherine responded. "I shall send one of the servants."

Elizabeth felt a surge of triumph. She smiled and bobbed a curtsey.

But Merrivale shook his head. "That won't be necessary," he said softly. "I need to visit the town. She can ride with me."

Elizabeth froze. She looked to Lady Catherine for support, but the lady's eyes were fixed on Merrivale, and she simply nodded. "As you wish," she said. "I can continue the painting without you now. Take good care of her."

"Oh, I shall," Merrivale replied, gracious as ever. "I cannot tell you how delighted I am that she is prepared to renounce her faith and family to join the true religion."

An hour later, Merrivale's elegant gray horse was ready. He mounted, and one of the grooms hoisted Elizabeth into the saddle behind him. She was obliged to ride squashed against his back, holding on to him so as not to fall. It was appalling to be so close to the man responsible for imprisoning her mother. She felt as though her hatred should burn him. She imagined it, willed it, that the strength of her feelings should poison him, infecting him as they rode away from the manor. But Merrivale gave no sign of it. He seemed remarkably cheerful, talking to his horse, fondly patting its graceful, muscled neck. He paid Elizabeth no attention at all.

It was a cold, bright morning. Frost melted in the fields, and as the gray horse splashed through the mud and puddles, Elizabeth tried to concentrate on her plan. Merrivale's attendance made things more difficult, but she had suspected he would not allow her to visit the town on her own. She pushed back her fears, the worries about her mother and brother, and thought hard about what she had to do.

Despite the promise to her father, Elizabeth was about to reveal the location of the old abbey's secret rooms to Thomas Montford. No one except she and her father and brother knew about the hidden places. Even her mother didn't know, though she was well aware that the family was custodian of a sacred trust. The secret was revealed only to direct descendants.

Among the hundreds of monks who had lived and worked and prayed in the abbey for the countless years before it was destroyed, there existed a small, secret sect. For generations the Dyer family had been servants to this inner order, the wisest and most learned of all the monks, who maintained a library of secret learning in chambers deep beneath the hill. When the abbey was disbanded, the library was kept safe. When Henry VIII sent his men to destroy the building, to pull down its walls stone by stone, to loot the gold from its treasury, the secret library was never discovered.

The monks of the inner order were now long dead. But the secret had remained with the Dyer family, who continued to protect the store of arcane and dangerous knowledge. And while rumors of the library's existence still floated about, only Edward and his two elder children knew the truth of the matter. Only they could find the path into the secret places beneath the hill.

How could the family pledge loyalty to the new Church of England when they were charged with such a trust, when they had served the old order so faithfully for generations? It was a sacred promise, a bond that could not be broken until such time as the Catholic Church held sway in England again and the abbey was restored to its former glory.

Elizabeth wrestled with her conscience. When her father had shown her the doorway, she had sworn on her life never to tell anyone—except her own children at the proper time. Now she was preparing to break this vow. Her stomach tightened as she thought about the gravity of her decision. The priest's mission was so important that Robert had been prepared to risk his life—all of their lives—to protect him. If Thomas could be hidden in the old library, he would be safe. And he could be trusted with this deepest of secrets—she was sure of that. But what if something went wrong? What if she inadvertently led Merrivale to the library? This possibility was too terrible to contemplate. She shuddered, and Merrivale sensed the movement, because he half turned his head.

"Are you cold?" he asked. "Shall I take you back to the manor?"

"No," Elizabeth said shortly, though in truth the icy air nipped her cheeks.

Merrivale laughed and clapped his heels against the horse's sides so that it jumped forward and set off at a brisk canter, obliging Elizabeth to hold on more tightly.

At last they reached the town. The horse clattered over the bridge and up the cobbled hill to the house on Silver Street. Elizabeth slid off. How long had she been away? No more than a few nights, but her home looked strange—cold and dark, untended, the windows grimy. Behind her, Merrivale dropped lightly to the ground.

Elizabeth tried the door, but it was bolted from the inside. So she hammered on it with her fist. "Esther! Mary!" she called. She heard a movement in the house, then eager voices. The bolt was drawn back, and there they stood.

A smile lit Esther's face—until she spotted Merrivale standing behind her sister. Her eyes widened, and she opened her mouth as though she was about to cry out, but Mary pulled her from the doorway, standing like a barricade between the girl and the man who had taken the mistress away. The old woman looked from Elizabeth to Merrivale, trying to understand what was happening. "Why is he here?" Mary said, her voice tremulous. "Is he taking the little one? What does he want?"

"Mary—no. He hasn't come for Esther. He wouldn't let me see you unless he accompanied me." Elizabeth glanced back at Merrivale, but he didn't speak. He simply stroked the face of the gray horse with his gloved hand.

Esther pushed past Mary and held out her arms to her sister. When Elizabeth scooped her up, Esther began to sob. "Where is Mum? I want Mum," she cried.

Elizabeth's heart seemed to melt in her chest. She stroked Esther's hair tenderly, but she couldn't surrender to her feelings. She rallied her strength. "How have you been?" she said over her sister's shoulder to Mary.

"We're bearing up," Mary said. "We're waiting for the mistress to be released. But don't worry about us. I can take care of Esther." She lifted Esther from her sister's embrace. Then she and Elizabeth exchanged a long, intense look. *We are together in this,* the look said. *I trust you to be strong. We can rely on each other.*

Elizabeth backed away. "I shall go to the chapel now," she said to Merrivale. She set off on foot, and he followed, leading the horse.

The broken walls of the old abbey loomed ahead, casting a chilly shadow over the town. The roof was gone, and many of the stones had been pillaged for new buildings, but three walls remained standing. Their empty, arched windows gave a view of clear sky. White doves and black crows nested in nooks in the stonework. Only one chapel of the old abbey remained whole, left to the town to serve the new Church of England, though the murals had been whitewashed and the forest of golden candlesticks harvested for the king's treasury.

The chapel stood in the shadows of the three ruined walls. Its doorway was vast, out of proportion to the size of the remaining building. Carved angels on each side of the archway climbed a ladder to heaven.

"Will the parish priest be here?" Merrivale asked.

Elizabeth nodded. In truth, she had no idea *where* the priest would be, but that did not stop her from speaking. "I understand he attends the church at noon for an hour, to advise his parishioners."

Merrivale shrugged. He did not look convinced.

"Do you intend to follow me, even into the chapel?" Elizabeth said primly.

"Of course," he replied, looping the reins of his horse on the church gate.

Elizabeth shrugged, but her heart was thundering. So much could go wrong.

They opened the door and stepped inside, and the cold gloom of the chapel swallowed them up. Rows of wooden pews streamed away from them to the bare stone altar at the front. Merrivale strolled up the aisle, brushing the end of each pew with his hand.

"There is no one here," he said. His voice was very loud, the words bouncing off the walls. But even as he spoke, a man in a dark robe stepped out of a doorway behind the altar. He nodded to them both as he approached.

Elizabeth could hardly breathe. The scene had a terrible unreality. Her mind whirled, but she forced herself to stand up straight. This was no time for her wits to desert her. She took a deep breath, preparing to make up another story, but the man spoke first.

"I am the deacon here. Are you a visitor to the town?"

Merrivale nodded, his eyes like dark stones as he stared at the deacon. "I am a servant of the queen," he said. "My name is Christopher Merrivale. This is Elizabeth Dyer. Perhaps you know her—a recalcitrant who does not attend your services . . . the daughter of a Catholic family. Now she thinks she will convert and wants your guidance."

The deacon turned to Elizabeth, examining her closely. "Is this true? Is it your wish to turn away from heresy, Elizabeth?"

She looked at the ground and nodded. The deacon seemed momentarily at a loss, not knowing what was expected of him, but Elizabeth piped up. "Will you tell me about the new prayer book?" she asked. "I need to understand how I can change myself, how I've been mistaken in my old beliefs."

"Of course. One moment, and I will get the book from the vestry," the deacon said. He gestured for the girl and her companion to be seated; then he disappeared through the door behind the altar.

Elizabeth sat down, but Merrivale remained standing. She sensed his irritation. He seemed to suspect she was up to something but didn't know what it was.

The deacon returned. He opened the Book of Common Prayer and began to read aloud.

Merrivale sighed with exasperation. Clearly he didn't want to listen to the man maunder on and on. "I shall wait outside the door," he told Elizabeth. "Don't try to leave on your own." With a scowl, he stomped out of the chapel. "You have half an hour," he called over his shoulder. The door slammed behind him.

The deacon stared at Elizabeth, and she stared at him. Then they laughed, a shared moment of strange, unsuitable mirth. There was no joy in it, just relief.

Elizabeth jumped to her feet. "We must be quick," she

said. "He might come in again." She led the priest to the east wall. "My father showed me this place on my tenth birthday," she whispered. "God help me, I swore I would never reveal the secret to anyone outside the family, even unto death."

Her fingers searched the rough stone in the fat pillar supporting an arch over the altar. She closed her eyes. *Forgive me, Lord,* she prayed. *And forgive me, Father, wherever you are.*

Thomas put his hand on her shoulder. "I shan't betray your trust," he said quietly.

Elizabeth's fingertips isolated a swirled nub of stone on either side of the pillar. She pressed them. Nothing happened. She pressed them again, harder, willing the door to open. It had been so long, perhaps the mechanism had seized up. "It's not working," she said. But as she spoke, there was a curious grinding within the giant pillar, and stones moved, pulling back to reveal a space barely wide enough for a man to slip through. Dark and chilly, the entrance gave off a breath of earth and ancient incense.

"There is a narrow stairway," Elizabeth said. "Go down, and you will find the old library. There is water . . . a well. We'll get food to you somehow."

"Man does not live on bread alone, but on every word that comes from the mouth of God," the priest said. "Won't you come with me, Elizabeth? I don't want to leave you with Merrivale."

Elizabeth shook her head. "If I disappear, what might he do to my mother or even Esther?" she said. "You go. Now. Hurry." The priest stepped into the dark space, and she pushed the nubs in the pillar again so that the stones slid back into place.

She returned to the pew and took up the book again just as Merrivale stormed into the chapel. He glared at her. "Where is he?" he yelled.

"The deacon? He told me he had to leave," Elizabeth said.

"There is no deacon." Merrivale spat out the words.

The parish priest stepped in behind Merrivale. Elizabeth had seen him often in the streets of Maumesbury, and she knew that he and Merrivale had met once before, when Isabella was captured. Her stomach clenched. Clearly the two men had been speaking outside the chapel.

"That is true," said the priest. "The parish does not have a deacon."

"Was it he? Was that Thomas Montford?" Merrivale demanded. He ran around the chapel, searching. He peered under the pews. He threw open the door to the vestry, disappeared inside for a moment, then returned, his face red and flustered.

"It is most strange," said the priest. "There is no other way to leave. If the man you seek had departed, you would have seen him."

Merrivale strode down the aisle to Elizabeth. "Where is he? Where did he go?" He raised a hand as though to strike her, but the parish priest rushed over.

"Stop!" he cried. "Not in the church!" He was wary of Merrivale, keeping a distance as he blustered his commands.

Merrivale cursed and stamped his foot. "To think he was here—right under my nose! Where did he go, Elizabeth? I'll have my men come and pull this place to pieces! I'll have them turn the town upside down! And you!" He glared at her. "What shall I do to you, you little witch!"

The priest clucked again, plump with outrage at this ungodly behavior in the church.

Merrivale drew himself up straight, looking as though he would gladly strangle the priest and Elizabeth after him. It was the first time she had seen him lose control. In the depths of her terror she felt a curious grain of triumph. She had beaten him.

16

Questions

Merrivale dragged Elizabeth out of the chapel. Behind them, the parish priest wrung his hands, protesting feebly. Elizabeth resisted, trying to pull free, struggling and batting at Merrivale with her hands, but he was strong and relentless. He jerked her through the doorway, and in the bright sunlight he struck her across the face with the back of his hand. Pain exploded in her head. The force of the blow knocked her to the ground. She felt the inside of her cheek tear on her teeth.

Elizabeth lay on the cold ground, stunned and gasping. Blood dripped from her mouth. She shook her head, trying to clear the white haze of pain fogging her thoughts. Slowly she clambered to her feet again, but Merrivale raised a fist and punched the side of her head. There was a white flash before her eyes, and suddenly everything seemed very distant—Merrivale, the broken abbey walls, the crows flapping from their high perches.

Merrivale pulled Elizabeth to her feet again. Dimly she wondered if he would strike her a third time. Instead, he dragged her away from the chapel along the path to the gate where his horse was tethered. He lifted her onto his shoulder and threw her over the horse's back. Then he swung into the saddle himself.

This time Elizabeth didn't have even the dignity of riding behind him. Instead, she lay on her belly across the front of the saddle, blood seeping out of her mouth, her ears ringing. Merrivale kicked the horse, turning it around; then he headed out of the town.

Elizabeth was horribly uncomfortable, slung over the horse. The blood that had leaked from her mouth congealed all over her face. Her head throbbed painfully, and she felt sick, her stomach churning and hot sweat breaking out all over her body. She tried to discern where they were going, but it was hard to see with her face pressed against the horse's shoulder. His hooves seemed frighteningly close, thundering over the ground beneath her.

The journey went on and on. Elizabeth lapsed into unconsciousness—whether for a few minutes or longer it was impossible to know—and when she came to, she began to retch. A thin stream of brown vomit flowed from her sore mouth to the muddy ground. Some caught on the horse's leg, and Merrivale cursed her, kicking at her with his boot.

When they stopped at last, daylight was fading, though the sky was still clear. A sunset broke over a copse of black trees like a yolk, silhouetting a large stone house. Merrivale called out, letting Elizabeth drop in a heap to the ground, where she remained, unable to move. In a moment the door opened, and two men ran out. Merrivale dismounted and stamped his feet to warm them; he barked orders. The first man took the reins of the horse. The second picked up Elizabeth and hurriedly carried her into the house. Merrivale followed them in and disappeared into one of the rooms, but all Elizabeth could see was the comforting blaze of a fire before the door was shut.

The man carried her up some stairs. He unlocked a door, maneuvered her into a room, and then dropped her on the floor. Without a word he went out, locking the door again.

Elizabeth lay exactly as she had fallen. After the long, bumpy, agonizing ride it was bliss for her tired, injured body just to be still. Her face hurt, but the knives of pain drew back a little if she didn't move. Far away she could hear men's voices, but nothing mattered anymore—not her family or the priest, not Isabella or Lady Catherine. Then darkness swallowed her up.

How long was she asleep? She had no idea, but it was still nighttime when the door opened and a man hauled her to her feet.

"Stand up," he said. "You're coming with me." It wasn't the man who had carried her inside, nor was it Merrivale. This one stank of beer and bad meat. He wasn't careful with her, half dragging her down the stairs to the room with the fire, leaving her to stand in front of a table. Merrivale sat on the other side. There were several other men lurking in the gloom, but Elizabeth couldn't tell how many. Merrivale looked sleek and warm, as though he had just enjoyed a hearty meal. He stretched out his legs, relaxed again, perfectly in control.

"Elizabeth," he said. "It's time we had a proper talk, you and I. That was a clever trick this afternoon. You surprised me, and I have no idea how you managed it. But it is only a brief setback. I have ordered men to search the chapel from top to bottom—and then the rest of the town. Your friend will not be safe for long."

Elizabeth tried to swallow. "May I have a drink, please?" she whispered.

Merrivale leaned forward, pretending he hadn't heard. "What did you say?"

"May I have a drink, please?"

He ignored her request. "This place," he said, gesturing around him, "has been entrusted to me for the carrying out of my duties, for the protection of the state, for . . . priest hunting. I must say I enjoyed the fine company at Spirit Hill, and it proved a good location in the searching out of secrets—your secrets. But this is a much more private and secluded place. No outsider can hear us. No one will interrupt us."

Elizabeth's head began to pound again. What would Merrivale and the other men do? The house was miles from anywhere. She was alone and at their mercy. They could do what they liked. She closed her eyes and prayed. *God, help me. Lord Jesus, help me. Holy Mother, help me now.*

With showy care Merrivale picked up a leather bag from the table and slowly took out a bundle of papers. He worked his way through them one by one, selecting a page with a flourish. "Ah," he said. "What have we here? Yes, a letter intercepted at Oxford, warning the heretic priest—one Thomas Montford—that he was about to be discovered, suggesting he flee with Robert Dyer, a Catholic sympathizer." He paused for a moment to give her a cold smile. Then he continued. "I think you know this traitor Robert Dyer."

Elizabeth rocked on her feet. The headache filled all the spaces of her mind, leaving her too little room to think. She didn't answer.

"Elizabeth," Merrivale said sharply. "This isn't simply a matter of private conscience. The queen herself has said she does not wish to make a window into men's souls. The priests coming from Spain and France want to start a Catholic uprising. They want to overthrow the rightful Queen of England. There have been attempts on her life."

His voice rose as he spoke, and now he sat forward in his chair, staring into her face.

Elizabeth stared back. The firelight played over him, and the shadows moved, gold and black and gold again.

"Where are they?" he demanded. "I need to find them— Dyer and Montford—and you know where they are."

A sigh escaped Elizabeth's lips. In the dark forest of her mind, a tiny light bloomed. They hadn't caught Robert! And Merrivale didn't know where he was. Robert was safe— somewhere. "May I have a drink?" she whispered again.

"Tell me where they're hiding, Elizabeth. You are a child. I know you're only caught up in this because of your brother. Why should you carry his burden? Tell me where he and the priest have gone, and I will set you free. And your mother as well."

"Where is she?" Elizabeth blurted out. "Is she here, too?"

Merrivale considered. "Yes, she's here," he said. "Would you like to see her?"

Elizabeth began to tremble. She wished she hadn't spoken. Was her mother really in the house, or was that a lie, a way to torment her into telling him what he wanted to know? She didn't answer the question.

"Do you think I enjoy this, Elizabeth? Being stuck here in the filthy country?" Merrivale sounded petulant now. "Wouldn't it be good if we could settle this matter? If I could get my hands on the priest and your brother, then I could let you and your mother go." Abruptly his voice changed. "That *was* Thomas Montford in the chapel this morning, wasn't it, Elizabeth?" he said harshly. "Tell me it was."

Elizabeth shook her head. "He said he was the deacon," she replied. Her voice croaked, and her mouth tasted rotten from the dried blood. She longed for a drink.

Merrivale yawned and lounged in his chair again, letting her see how comfortable he was, letting her know he had all the time in the world.

The questions went on and on. Elizabeth was obliged to stand, and Merrivale wouldn't give her a drink. He asked her about her brother and his friends, about her family and the fines they paid for not attending church. He even asked her about Lady Catherine—how long Elizabeth had worked for her, what they talked about, what Elizabeth knew about Lord Cecil. He repeated the same questions over and over. Once, when she didn't answer fast enough, he began to shout. Then he was gentle, pouring water into a cup for her to drink, holding the vessel to her lips as the water soaked into her parched mouth.

She told him a great deal—but nothing, *nothing,* about Robert or Thomas. Finally, Merrivale ordered one of his men to take her back to the room. They would talk again soon, he said. She would tell him what he wanted to know in the end.

The man who smelled of bad meat hauled her up the stairs and locked the door behind her. It was cold and dark in the room. A raw draft blew through the bare floorboards. The shutters were nailed closed over the window. Elizabeth curled up, clasping her legs, trying to pray, but her thoughts were in disarray. Merrivale's voice echoed in her head, and it was hard to remember what she had told him.

Sometime later the door opened. Had they come to fetch her already? Elizabeth was flooded with dread. But it seemed they hadn't come for her. Instead, a woman was shoved through the door.

Elizabeth sat up straight. Her mouth dropped open. "Mother?" she said. "Is that you?"

The woman raised a hand to her face, eyes wide. "Elizabeth! What are you doing here?" she cried. "Why are you here?"

Elizabeth stood up, and the two embraced, both shaking all over. They pulled back and stared at each other, mother and daughter, the pleasure of the reunion overshadowed by a dread of the circumstances in which they found themselves.

Elizabeth searched her mother's face, and her heart ached. How tired Jane looked. How gaunt and old and beaten down. "Mum—did they hurt you?" she asked.

"No, they only questioned me and locked me up. How many days has it been, Elizabeth? I've lost count. I was so afraid for you and—"

Quickly, Elizabeth raised a finger to her lips, certain that someone would be listening.

Jane nodded, understanding Elizabeth's caution. Tears welled in her eyes. "They hurt you," she whispered, gently touching the bruise on Elizabeth's face. "What are we going to do? If they threaten to hurt you again, what will I do?"

"I think that's why they brought me here," Elizabeth whispered back. She rested her forehead on her mother's shoulder. They sat down together in the cold, bare room, arms around each other. Fingers of light poked through the shutters. Outside, birds began to sing, and wind stirred the trees. Then she heard voices and the staccato of hooves.

She peered out through the chinks in the covered window and saw Merrivale riding away. Was this a good sign? Where was he going?

They were left alone. A leather bucket was provided as a chamber pot, and in the middle of the day, a plate of boiled barley, gray and congealed, was shoved through the door. But neither Elizabeth nor her mother had an appetite. The time stretched out, empty hours in which to brood about the prospect of Merrivale's return and another interrogation. They tried to keep their spirits up, whispering together, reciting the rosary, singing little songs. They talked about Esther and Mary, and Elizabeth told her mother about the recent days at the manor, about Isabella getting scrubbed and Lady Catherine painting Merrivale's portrait. But she did not say one word about Robert or the priest.

Merrivale returned just before sunset, accompanied by the man he had first brought with him to Spirit Hill. Elizabeth and Jane peered through the shutters. Both riders were filthy from their journey, and Merrivale was angry, doling out curses at his servants when they came out to greet him. The row continued as the men entered the house. There were loud voices and the sounds of a struggle of some kind.

Elizabeth and her mother regarded each other in horror. Merrivale's rage didn't bode well. If he lashed out at his men, what would he do to them? They waited, nerves taut, for the door to be unlocked and the inevitable questioning to begin. But unexpectedly, the uproar died down, and the odors of cooking drifted through the house. Merrivale was settling down to eat.

An hour or so crept past, and the waiting was a torment in itself. Fear gnawed, never letting go. Merrivale would call for them to be brought down sooner or later, and there was no telling what might happen then. Judging from his temper, his patience had worn very thin.

A beam of yellow light leaked into the room. Elizabeth pressed her face to the rough shutter to see a huge, fiery moon rising over the trees. It was remarkable . . . beautiful. For a moment the spectacle distracted her—the trees, perfectly still, pointing their spiky black hands at a moon that burned.

She turned back to the room—and blinked. The light was shifting, throwing shadows awry. Particles of dust began to spin in coils, and the house creaked suddenly, seemed to move, like an old woman shifting her aching joints.

"What is it?" Jane said.

Elizabeth shook her head. "I don't know."

They both lifted their faces, trying to sense . . . what?

The house groaned. The walls seemed to swell and bulge. The stones glistened.

17

The Summoning

sabella spent the morning after her trip to the woods scrubbing her clothes. Lady Catherine had been furious when she'd woken to find her newly clean charge plastered in filth. "Where did you go?" she asked. "After all the time we spent cleaning you yesterday! Look at your gown! How ungrateful! After all we have done for you."

Isabella stared at Lady Catherine's feet and tried to let the words wash over her. But she wasn't entirely impervious. Lady Catherine's anger was fierce as a whip. A tear leaked from her eye. "I'm sorry," she whispered. "I'm very sorry."

Lady Catherine pulled up, hearing the apology. Perhaps she was glad Isabella had come back at all, after her mysterious night jaunt. The girl might have simply run away for good.

"I'm not used to living like this," Isabella said, spreading her arms wide. Her gesture seemed to encompass everything—the house, the people, her clothes.

Lady Catherine sighed and nodded. "I do understand. But don't go out again," she said. "You are not to live like an animal any longer, Isabella. You are a Christian, and you must stay with us."

Isabella washed herself with a cloth and a basin of water. Then, as a punishment, she was sent to the kitchen to heat a vat of water and wash her dirty clothes. At least that meant she could pass Elizabeth and let her know with a smile that she had done as she'd promised.

The dour cook gave Isabella instructions and inspected her work. Mud from the woods had badly stained Isabella's white shift, warm gown, and overskirt. The washing seemed to take forever. She was on her knees in the kitchen, elbow-deep in warm water, when she heard a horse at the front of the house. She stood up and looked out the window.

"It's the Catholic girl, going off with Master Merrivale," the cook said. "Perhaps he's going to lock her up." She sniffed and wiped her nose. "High time," she added disapprovingly.

Isabella couldn't understand why Elizabeth was riding behind Kit Merrivale. The sight filled her with dismay. Was her friend under arrest? Had the priest been found out? When she and Elizabeth had concocted the plan the previous night, they had assumed that one of the servants would be ordered to accompany Elizabeth to the town. They had not imagined Merrivale would bother to take her.

The cook grunted, indicating that Isabella should return to her washing. Isabella dropped to her knees again, mashing and swishing the stained, sodden fabric in the bucket, but her thoughts raced. She had a bad feeling, seeing Elizabeth ride away with her enemy. Lady Catherine had provided Elizabeth with a degree of protection, but once out of the lady's sight, what might Merrivale do?

All sorts of terrible possibilities loomed in her mind. She hurried her task. When the clothes were washed, rinsed, wrung, and hung up to dry, she trotted from the kitchen to Lady Catherine's workroom. Outside the door, she took a deep breath, checked her cap, and stood up straight. She knocked.

"Enter," the lady called.

Isabella opened the door and stepped into the room. The portrait of Kit Merrivale was well advanced now. Lady Catherine had worked fast. The face was finished, though the background and the rich fabrics of the sitter's clothing were yet to be filled in. Still, Isabella was stunned. She had never seen anything like it. The quality of the likeness was astonishing. The very soul of Kit Merrivale stared from his portrait—handsome and sly, ambitious and intelligent, clever and cruel. Yes, even his cruelty was depicted, in the lines of his mouth, in the cold eyes and their careful consideration of the viewer. Isabella shivered.

"What is it?" Lady Catherine asked, a trace of annoyance in her voice at the interruption.

"I wonder if you would tell me where Elizabeth has gone," Isabella said.

Lady Catherine lifted her brush from the canvas and looked at Isabella thoughtfully. "She's gone to the town," she said. "Kit has taken her. Are you friends now, you two?"

"Yes," Isabella said.

Lady Catherine turned back to her painting. "Don't worry, she'll return later," she said. "She wanted to see her sister, poor girl. She's missing her family."

Isabella spent the rest of the day worrying, desperate to

see her friend return. She was called upon to help the little maid, Deb, clean the hearths and spread fresh rushes on the floor. Deb chattered on, but Isabella felt painfully shy, and her thoughts were bound up with Elizabeth.

At the end of the afternoon, as the light faded, Lady Catherine began to worry, too. "They should have returned by now. Where are they?" she fretted.

The sun descended. The men of the house gathered in the long hall, waiting for their evening meal. Eventually, irritable at the delay, Lady Catherine gave up and ordered the meal to be served. She insisted Isabella sit beside her, and she filled their plates, though neither of them had the appetite to eat very much. Afterward, they sat by the fire, still waiting, till past ten o'clock.

When Lady Catherine finally sent Isabella to bed, she patted her on the head. "Try not to fret. I'm sure there's a perfectly good reason why they haven't returned," she said.

Isabella nodded, managing a little smile. But she was not reassured. She curled up on her mattress in the corridor as the rest of the household settled down to sleep. All through the long hours of darkness she lay awake, her eyes fixed on the ceiling. Elizabeth was in danger; she was sure of it.

Late the next morning Merrivale returned alone. He looked tired, and his face was dark. Lady Catherine ran out of the house when he arrived, ran right up to him, dodging his horse's hooves. "Where have you been?" she cried. "Where's Elizabeth? What have you done with her?"

Hearing the voice of their mistress, the servants all looked out, craning their necks to see what was going on.

"Making a fool of herself over that young man," the cook muttered, loud enough for everyone to hear. "*And* making a fuss over the Catholic girl. Good riddance, I say."

Outside, Merrivale tugged savagely at the reins so that his horse backed up abruptly, throwing its head in the air. He swung his leg over the horse's withers and slid to the ground, then threw the reins to a groom who had come running from the stables.

"Kit, please," Lady Catherine said, laying her hand on his arm. "What happened? Where's Elizabeth?"

Merrivale didn't answer. He jerked away and marched into the house. Lady Catherine trotted after him. Once inside, he threw down his whip with a clatter, dropped his sodden cloak to the floor, pulled up a chair by the fire, and bawled for a servant to come pull off his boots.

Isabella hurried in, with a cup of warm beer and a bowl of porridge left over from breakfast.

"Kit," Lady Catherine persisted, hovering around him, pleading for his attention. "You must tell me what has happened."

He picked up the cup and took a long drink. Then he stared at Lady Catherine. "He was in the chapel, and I let him get away. I didn't recognize him! And she was so cool. God's blood! How did she do it, the filthy Catholic witch? How did she organize it? That's what I don't understand. And where did he go? He just vanished."

Lady Catherine recoiled, stunned by the venom in his voice. "I don't understand. What are you talking about?" she asked.

"I'm talking about Elizabeth. Your *dear* girl is a traitor

and a heretic," he said. "And you've sheltered her in your home while she plotted against the queen."

"What?" Lady Catherine flapped her hands in front of her face as if trying to push his words away.

Neither she nor Merrivale paid attention to Isabella, waiting with the porridge bowl. It was just as well, for her hands were shaking. From what Merrivale had said, it seemed the priest had escaped. But where was Elizabeth?

"She's under arrest," Merrivale said, as if reading Isabella's thoughts. "I will need all of your men to search the town. The Catholic priest is still there—somewhere. I'll tear the whole place down to find him, if need be."

"Of course, if you must." Lady Catherine was distracted, wringing her hands. Her eyes were full of tears. "Please . . . please tell me what happened," she said.

Merrivale was still fuming. "One of your servants is helping her," he said. "Someone here at Spirit Hill. How else could she have organized the meeting?"

Lady Catherine shook her head. "No. The other servants keep their distance. She is shunned because of her faith."

"And yet she managed to draw *you* in, Catherine. You made her a friend. Why is that? Shall I have you arrested, too?"

Lady Catherine was horrified. She stretched out a hand to Merrivale, grasping his arm. "You wouldn't!" she said. "I thought . . . I thought we were friends, Kit. Why are you saying this? You know I'm not a traitor!"

Merrivale clenched his fist and pulled away. His face was full of pent-up rage and frustration. He looked like a child caught in a fit of anger, albeit one with recourse to boots and fists and with the power to order arrest, imprisonment, and torture.

Isabella wanted to run away, to leave the house far behind and return to the crow people and the safety of the shadow world. Her heart was thundering, and he would hear it, surely, and suspect that she was the one who had conspired with Elizabeth. And what about Lady Catherine? Would she remember that Isabella had gone out the night before and realize that she could have been the messenger?

Kit suddenly turned to Isabella. "Come here," he commanded. Isabella let out a small frightened sound, but Merrivale simply seized the bowl of porridge. He took a large spoonful, and grimaced. "Filthy stuff," he said.

Lady Catherine stared at him, tearful and shocked. "I thought I meant something to you, Kit," she said. "We enjoyed each other's company. We talked."

Isabella could hardly bear to look at the lady. She appeared old and shrunken, her pride sucked out of her.

Merrivale was oblivious. Despite his earlier complaint, he ate greedily. "Leave me," he said. "I have the queen's authority, Catherine. Her protection is my first priority. Nothing else matters. Do you understand?"

Lady Catherine backed away, gathering her dignity. She dropped Merrivale a cold curtsey and stalked out of the room. But once through the door, she picked up her skirts and ran up the stairs. Isabella hurried after, but Lady Catherine had locked the door behind herself. Isabella could hear her sobbing.

The early evening was eerie and melancholy. A gloom settled over the branches of the bare trees as Isabella walked away from the house, across a field, to a solitary hawthorn in a hedgerow of ash and elm. She didn't hesitate. She didn't look over her shoulder. There was no going back now. Elizabeth was in peril, and Isabella had to try to save her.

She took a deep breath and pulled off her white woolen cap. The cold air prickled her scalp, teasing her cropped hair. Isabella had wanted to find her brother and bring him with her to live in the ordinary world, to leave the crow people behind. Now she was turning to them for help—as her mother had so many years before. What choice had her mother had then? What choice did she have now? None. None at all.

A haze of red berries still adorned the hawthorn tree, though its branches were leafless and black. The hawthorn— beloved by the crow people, because it sent roots into the ordinary world *and* into the faerie world. Isabella shivered, sensing invisible shadows falling about her. She circled the tree once, twice. Half a dozen crows were perched on the branches of a nearby ash tree. They cawed and flapped their wings as Isabella walked around the hawthorn a third time.

The gloom deepened, but at the same time, features of the landscape seemed to gain intensity. The last rays of sunlight sparkled on the tips of trees. Stones gleamed underfoot like gems.

Isabella called out a name in a loud, fierce voice. The crows cawed again, angry now, and flew away in a clatter. Darkness gathered like skirts around Isabella and the bent, red-veiled tree. Something stirred in the mass of branches— a movement like an old woman turning over in her sleep. There was a puff of cold, sweet air . . . the sound of voices far away. Isabella called out again the long, complex name that echoed across the fields.

The stones underfoot began to move as if the summoning had disturbed them. Then a dark shape crossed the sky, blotting out the light. Huge black wings beat with a sound of thunder. A hoarse call broke the air above Isabella's head. She raised her arms—her emotions a storm of fear, excitement, and triumph—and laughed out loud.

The faerie landed beside her, his fierce claws, daggered with gray talons, lightly touching the ground. He was mostly bird now, a huge crow with glossy feathers. His face was beaked, his eyes bright gold. He looked at Isabella, turning his head to one side. She stepped closer and carefully climbed on his back. The feathers were cold and smooth. She pressed her body beneath them, so that only her head was visible against the body of the faerie.

"Can you find her?" she asked. The faerie dipped his head. She didn't have to explain. There was a bond between them still. She held on tight as the crow man spread his great wings and rose into the air.

18

Dark Angels

homas Montford stood in the dark. The stone door had closed behind him, cutting off all light and sound from the chapel. It was utterly black. The curious perfume of dead flowers filled his lungs. He could taste dust on his tongue, could feel it settling on his face. He hardly dared to move, but he lifted his arms and encountered the narrow curved walls of the pillar. The space was like a tomb.

Thomas gasped for air. The darkness was oppressive, and he sensed the crushing weight of stone over his head. He wondered what was happening outside, what Elizabeth was doing, and realized he could do nothing for her now. He shut his eyes and tried to breathe evenly. *Dear God,* he prayed, *guide me now. Help me find the way.*

He had to move, had to find the stairway. He shifted one foot, blindly feeling for the edge of the step. There—there it was, the stone giving way to empty space. Slowly, cautiously, he lowered his foot to the next step, keeping one arm against the wall. Down he went again, feeling his way, step by step, on a steep spiral staircase.

It was a long descent, and after a while Thomas began to feel dizzy. He clutched the wall with both hands, leaning his back against it, afraid he would fall. Then the wall itself seemed to reel away, and it was hard to tell if he was upright or lying down, standing or falling into space. Despite the cold air, he broke out in a hot sweat. Dust tickled his nose, and he sneezed—the sound echoing over and over, bouncing off the stone coil of the staircase.

He had to move on. Down he went, beneath the church . . . under soil and rock, the buried flints of the ancients, the forgotten coins of the Romans . . . down into the bowels of the hill. The staircase ended abruptly at a wooden door that Thomas walked into with a bump. It was a relief—and a shock. He spread his hands and ran his fingers over its surface till he found a simple iron latch, which he lifted.

As Thomas stepped into the room, a warm white light flared from a stone bowl that rested on a table. He drew a breath, staring in wonder. A pearly ball rose from the bowl and seemed to spin, casting light as it moved. Slowly, dazzled by the brightness, he stretched out his hand to it, but he felt neither heat nor cold. And when he reached out to clasp the ball, it dropped away—only to rise again when he withdrew his hand.

Thomas was fascinated. What had created such a thing? It crossed his mind that the device might be magical—and possibly demonic. But he pushed this consideration aside. After all, he was in the heart of the old abbey, where the Roman Catholic church had set up an inner circle of its most accomplished and devoted servants. At the seminary in Douai, there had been whispers about the powers of these monks. There were rumors that Maumesbury Abbey had once had such a closed circle, but Thomas hadn't credited them. Never had he thought he might see for himself what could be achieved by such men.

Magic might be allowed in such circumstances. After all, the three magi who visited the Christ child had foreseen the future and read the stars. But only the very few, the wisest and most learned, could meddle in such matters. The rest of humanity, the ordinary, ignorant rabble, had to be kept safe from such dangers and temptations.

Thomas stretched out his hand again, pleased by the white light and the graceful way it danced away from him. He was filled with excitement now. What other marvels might he find? By the uncanny light, the room was revealed to be circular and empty, except for the table. There was a second door opposite the one he had entered by. It wasn't locked, and when Thomas pulled it open, the ball of light followed him into the next chamber, floating just an arm's length away.

This second room was huge, wider than Thomas was able to see in his pool of magic light. And heaped on the floor, just in front of him, was a marvelous, haphazard pile of the old church's treasure. He saw fat gold candlesticks, chalices spotted with bright jewels, statues of the saints and the Virgin Mary inlaid with blue lapis lazuli and silvery mother-of-pearl. There were giant books bound with soft leather and encrusted with precious stones, tapestries of fine silk woven with threads of gold.

Staring at the careless pile, Thomas was stunned. Never, *never* had he seen anything like this. He stepped closer, crunching underfoot a rosary strung with beads of topaz and beryl. When the order for closure had come, when King Henry had demanded that Maumesbury Abbey be destroyed, the secret order must have hidden their most precious treasures in this place. Thomas imagined the scene: the monks feverishly gathering as much as they could, grabbing candlesticks, tearing down tapestries, while men on horseback carried the paper with the king's seal across the country. And then the few who knew the hiding place would have locked up the church, carried the treasure down the precipitous stairway, and dumped it in a heap on the cold ground. And here it had lain, all these decades, buried in darkness.

Was King Henry angry when the real treasures could not be found and he had to make do with the second best to fatten his coffers? Thomas smiled as he bent down to pick up a golden cup, still yellow as butter. It was simple, without any engraving or jeweled ornament, smooth and heavy in his hand. He put the cup down and began to explore the rest of the room. Like the first, it was circular. Deep wooden shelves covered the walls, and books filled the shelves. Few were as gaudy as those on the floor. These volumes, from all over Europe, the Far East, and North Africa, were plain and workmanlike. Mathematics, medicine, geography, language, architecture, and science. Thomas drew a few from a shelf and glanced at their pages. His heart quickened. How good it was, how marvelous, that such a wealth of books had survived.

But there was more to see. He proceeded to a smaller room beyond the library. Here he found a spring bubbling up into a basin carved in the stony floor. This must be the well Elizabeth had mentioned. He stooped to take a drink, clearing the taste of dust from his mouth. The water was achingly cold. He moved on again, and the path grew more complex. He passed through long corridors, peered into tiny cavelike rooms, several of which had simple beds inside. The passageways twisted and turned, sometimes surprising him by looping back to the spring or terminating suddenly. Always the magic light hovered around him, casting long shadows in the cold, dark tunnels. And it was *very* cold.

The longer Thomas walked, the colder he became, as though the rock walls were sucking the heat from his body. Perhaps, like the labyrinth devised by Daedalus in ancient Crete, the passageways were designed to trick and trap visitors. He judged that it might be wise to return to the relative safety of the library.

He headed back the way he had come, taking long strides, the ball of light easily keeping up. The corridor veered right and then left. Ahead he saw a large door in a Gothic arch, ornately decorated with wrought iron. He pulled up short. He hadn't seen this before! He hesitated for a moment. He had decided not to be lured by the maze, to go back to the library, but the grandeur of the door appealed to him. What lay beyond it? The handle was a large black ring, and Thomas could not resist it. He turned the ring, which lifted a latch on the other side. Then he pushed the door open and stepped inside.

It was a chapel, with half a dozen rows of carved wooden benches. At the far end stood a stone altar covered by a white cloth embroidered with stalks of ripe wheat and red poppies. On a high shelf behind the altar, twelve candles burned with magic white light. Next to them was a monstrance—a sunburst of beaten gold on a stand embedded with rubies. The vessel was intended to display Communion bread, and indeed, it contained the Holy Sacrament.

Overwhelmed, Thomas dropped to his knees and crossed himself. A stream of grateful words tumbled in his head, prayers of thanks to God. Then he looked up—and saw the paintings that covered the walls.

Across the land, churches had been stripped during the Reformation. People did not want the gaudy decorations of ancient times; they wanted simplicity, and many fine pictures had been covered in whitewash. But that hadn't happened here. The paintings in the secret chapel had survived. The pale, benevolent face of the Virgin Mary smiled down on him. Her head was haloed with gold, and in her lap, a chubby Christ child raised his infant hand in blessing. Beside her stood Saint Joseph, the shepherds, and the three wise men.

Thomas turned to see more. Yes, as he'd expected, there were the archangels in the scene on the facing wall: Saint Michael, clad in armor, with a sword in his hand and the dragon, Lucifer, at his feet; Saint Gabriel, holding a white lily; and Saint Raphael, bearing a pilgrim's staff.

The archangels were beautiful, with their white wings and gentle, luminous faces, and all about them another host of angels gathered. But these angels did not look gentle. They were tall and slender, and the wings sprouting from their backs were covered with black feathers. Their faces were fierce and angular, with bright golden eyes. Long ebony hair spilled from their heads, and they wore a multitude of dull golden bands—bracelets, rings, collars, and crowns. They were beautiful, too, Thomas thought, but as a barren desert was beautiful, or a wild moor covered in perfect white snow. Not a beauty to bring comfort. The painting pricked something inside him, filling him with a strange mixture of sadness and elation. Who had painted these creatures? What had inspired the artist to include them on the chapel wall in this holy place?

Thomas rose and stepped closer. The angels towered above him as he searched around their long white feet for a name or a symbol that might identify the artist. He continued looking for a clue, until, with a shock, he came face to face with someone he recognized. Standing among the dark angels but reaching only half their height, peeping out from the forest of their limbs and wings, was a green girl. Her eyes peered from the painting into his.

Thomas stepped back in fright. His heart beat so loudly it seemed to echo in the silent chapel. The magic candles guttered. It was uncanny how accurately the artist had captured the face, the gentle expression, and the small, strong body. Thomas stared. How? How could this be? The chapel beneath the hill had been locked up decades before Isabella was born. And why would she be painted among a host of angels? Thomas shivered, and tears pricked his eyes. He tried to master his emotions, to stay in control. It *couldn't* be Isabella. That was impossible. The painting was a fantastic coincidence and nothing more.

The priest tore himself away and continued his inspection. The scene ended strangely, with a painting of a tall, empty archway. Beneath it, the name of the artist was recorded: *Jerome*. Thomas shivered again. So the painting of Isabella—except that it couldn't be Isabella—wasn't decades old. It was centuries old.

Thomas knew something of Jerome, the Maumesbury saint, and Robert had told him stories, too. Jerome had lived in the thirteenth century, and a hundred years after his death, he had been made a saint for his religious poetry and writings. He had lived alone for most of his life in the cell by the spring in the forest, connected to the abbey but not a part of it. Clearly he had been a member of the secret inner order, and he had decorated the chapel with his vision of angels. And with a green girl, too—a girl who looked just like Isabella Leland, who had taken Thomas, by coincidence, to hide in Jerome's old hermitage. The thought was nagging: Why was the girl in the picture?

Thinking about Isabella made Thomas think about Elizabeth. If her role in his escape had been uncovered, there was no telling what the priest hunter might do to her. Thomas was a naturally active man, and his helplessness now infuriated him. He depended so much on others, and so many had suffered to keep him safe. He had to remind himself that God would reward them for it. And the work had to be done, for the sake of the immortal souls of all the English people. He had to go on.

His mind in turmoil, Thomas made his way back to the library, guided by the magic light. Putting aside the burden of his worries, he centered his thoughts on the riddle of the green girl. He scoured the shelves for the writings of Saint Jerome and found them at last—a study of religious philosophy, an examination of the teachings of Jesus, a collection of poetry, and a plain, battered leather book containing the hermit's other religious writings. Thomas opened the book and brushed the surface of the fragile pages with his finger-tips. Then he began to read.

19

Goblins

sabella and the crow man flew across a landscape of fields, forests, and huddled dwellings. They traveled fast, and now and then traversed the boundaries of the shadow land, where the snow lay deep and bright fires burned in rings of stone. Once, she glimpsed a creature with a man's face and a stag's horns playing a black violin. Three stray, shrill notes reached her ears. Then the shadow land vanished, and the pastures returned . . . the bare trees . . . the byres where cows huddled against the cold.

The faerie screeched as it circled over a house at the edge of a spinney.

"Is she here? Is this the place?" Isabella called. She could hardly speak, her lips were so cold. The faerie dipped a wing, and Isabella clung tightly as they plummeted toward the earth. The ground rose so fast, she squeezed her eyes shut in fright. But the faerie landed lightly and shivered her off its back. Then it took off again and alighted on the tiled roof. Isabella hopped from one foot to another, waiting for the faerie to make its move. Was Elizabeth truly inside the house? The shutters were closed, but certainly there were people in the downstairs rooms. Chinks of light escaped from the windows, and smoke rose from the stone chimney.

The faerie leaped into the air. Its body broke up into a host of tiny pieces, each of which took on a life of its own and scampered across the roof. The little creatures—maybe three dozen of them—moved very quickly, and each found a way into the house. Some jumped down the chimney. Others lifted roof tiles and squeezed inside. Several scurried down the walls of the house and pushed through the shuttered windows. Dark and curiously shaped, the faerie creatures squeaked and gibbered to each other, perhaps still sensing they were parts of one being. Then they were gone, all of them, inside the house.

For a few moments everything was still and silent. Isabella held her breath, waiting to see what would happen.

Downstairs a man cried out. Elizabeth crossed the room and pressed her ear to the door. It sounded as though someone was tipping over the furniture. There were shouts . . . a clash, perhaps of blade against stone.

"Elizabeth," Jane said. "Come sit beside me. Now." Her voice was low and serious.

Elizabeth turned and dropped to a crouch beside her mother. A shadow passed in front of the shutter. A ribbon of scent tickled her nose, a weaving of church stone, incense, dying roses, cold earth.

Jane gripped her hand tightly. "There's something in the room," she whispered. "I saw it—in the shadows."

Elizabeth swallowed, straining her eyes. "Was it a rat?" she asked.

"No, no. Not a rat."

Downstairs the chaos continued—shouts among the men, and the sound of a struggle. Doors banged.

Elizabeth had never been so frightened, even in her encounters with Merrivale. The atmosphere of the house was unnatural. Something terrible was happening, a nightmare, and she didn't know what it was. That was the worst thing of all.

"There it is," Jane said. She stretched out a trembling hand and pointed to the corner of the room.

In the gloom one darker shadow moved and became distinct. Two round yellow eyes gleamed. The creature stepped forward into a pool of moonlight. It was about knee high, with a large pointed head and a skinny body. Its face was squashed, with heavy brows; a long, bent nose; and a tiny mouth over which two uneven teeth protruded. The expression in its eyes was hard to fathom.

"It's a goblin. A boggart," Jane moaned. "Horrible . . . evil . . . the devil's work!" She made the sign of the cross, but the goblin stayed where it was.

Jane's words set Elizabeth's thoughts ticking. An idea dawned. Might Isabella have something to do with the goblin's appearance?

Jane rose unsteadily to her feet, rallying her courage. "Stay where you are, Elizabeth. I'll see it off. I'll kick it—stamp on it." She drew back a foot, but Elizabeth reached out to stop her.

"No!" she said. "Leave it. Don't hurt it. I think . . . I think it might want to help us."

"Help us?" Jane said, dismayed. "That little devil? Why?"

The goblin turned its gnarled face to Elizabeth and blinked. Slowly it raised its left hand.

"It *is* going to help us," Elizabeth whispered. She reached out and took the goblin's clawed hand in her own. The goblin nodded and led her to the door. It passed its fingers over the latch, and they heard the bolt on the other side drop with a thud to the floor. The door swung open.

Isabella heard a bang and men shouting, then a clatter as furniture was knocked over. She ran up to the front of the house and peered into the dim room through the chinks in the shutters. She couldn't quite make out what was happening, but the faerie was certainly creating chaos. The men were frightened and called out to each other, crashing about and trying to maim or trample the horde of goblins rampaging through the house.

The shutters flew open, whacking Isabella in the face. She was knocked from her feet and fell onto her bottom on the cold grass. Blood dripped from her nose, but she hardly felt the pain. A particularly hideous goblin leered at her through the open window, hopping up and down on the sill. Mossy green and brown, its skin gnarled and knotted, the goblin looked like an old branch with twiggy fingers. Suddenly, a large brown jug was hurled through the air, skimming the goblin's head, to smash on the ground just an arm's length from Isabella. Despite everything, she erupted with laughter, and the goblin laughed, too, its crooked grin almost cutting its face in half. It winked a yellow eye, turned on its heels, and dived back into the room.

Isabella climbed to her feet, dabbing her nose on her sleeve. The front door flew open, and a man ran out of the house. His clothes were torn, and he was screaming. Isabella drew back, hoping he wouldn't see her, but she needn't have worried. The man was intent on escape. His legs flailed about in the mud, and he stumbled, all in a panic, to get away from the house and the imps.

Isabella laughed again, right to the depths of her belly. It made her feel good, though she wondered if it was a little wicked to find a man's terror so funny. Then again, this was one of Merrivale's men—and what sort of person would follow *him?* Surely not a kind and gentle one! Then it flashed into her mind that Elizabeth was somewhere in the house, and that *she* might not find the goblins as amusing as Isabella did.

She crept to the open door and looked inside. It was hard to see much, as the candles were all snuffed out and smoking. Most of the noise came from a room to the left—the one Isabella had spied on through the shutters. A staircase rose in front of her. Isabella hesitated, wondering where Elizabeth might be. She didn't want to run into Merrivale. Slowly she moved forward, trying to breathe evenly, wishing her heart wouldn't race.

There was a movement on the stair, and she froze. She heard a soft voice and a hiss. "Elizabeth?" she whispered. "Is that you?" Two bright yellow eyes shone from the stairway, and a goblin stepped forward, leading Elizabeth by the hand. Elizabeth's mother, Jane, followed close behind, clinging to her daughter's arm.

The two girls stared at each other. Isabella could hardly

believe her eyes. They had only been apart a day and a night—but how long those hours had been.

"Isabella!" Elizabeth said. "I knew it was you." She pushed forward and threw her arms around Isabella's neck. "Thank you. Thank you for coming to get us."

Isabella untangled herself. "Quickly! We must leave at once," she said.

Too late. The door to the side room flew open, and a man stumbled out and fell against Jane. Hard on his heels came Merrivale, shouting and swearing. He stopped short, staring at the fugitives as though he couldn't believe his eyes.

"God's wounds!" he cried. "Grab them, man. Don't let them escape." The first man lurched toward Isabella and grabbed her arm. Merrivale seized Elizabeth by the hair. He was sweating and wild-eyed, breathing heavily. "So *you* are the little accomplice," he said to Isabella. "How did you find your way here?"

But Merrivale didn't get the chance to interrogate the girls further. He was jerked back into the room by unseen hands. At the same time, Elizabeth's goblin sank its fangs into the flesh of her captor's leg. The man screeched and backed away, following Merrivale, but he kept his grip on Isabella and dragged her with him.

"Go! Run!" Isabella shouted. She knew the faerie would come to her aid, and she wanted Elizabeth and her mother to escape while they had the chance.

The room was full of movement. Goblins were climbing the walls and prancing on the edge of the overturned table. Two of the creatures were jumping up and down among the flames in the fireplace. Four more had pinned one of

Merrivale's men to the ground, and one danced on top of him. Another man, young and greasy-haired, was apparently under a spell, believing a particularly evil-looking one-eyed goblin to be his sweetheart. He was weeping as he clutched the simpering goblin's hand to his heart.

Isabella laughed again. She couldn't help it. She wasn't afraid. How ridiculous these men truly were, even Merrivale. But hearing her, Merrivale turned with a howl of rage. He drew a short, slim dagger from his sleeve and threw it—straight at her heart.

"Run, Elizabeth!" Jane had urged when Isabella was dragged through the door into the side room. "You heard what she said. We have to go now!" She tried to pull her daughter away, but Elizabeth dug in her heels.

"I'm not leaving Isabella! We have to help her!" she cried, breaking free. She stepped through the doorway just in time to see a thin silver knife fly from Merrivale's hand toward Isabella.

Elizabeth screamed in horror, expecting to see the deadly blade bury itself in Isabella's chest. But it never happened. The dagger stopped in midair, pointing at her friend's heart like a sharp, silver finger.

Isabella gasped. For an endless moment, she didn't move, as if waiting for the dagger to pierce her. But it hovered where it was, and at last she simply stepped away from it.

Suddenly, Elizabeth noticed how silent the house had become. She glanced around the room. Nothing was moving! Merrivale was frozen, his hand still outstretched from releasing the dagger. The goblins were motionless, too, caught in a variety of curious postures all over the room—laughing, jumping, climbing. One had thrown a clay cup in the air, and it hung there still, just beneath the ceiling. Even the flames in the fireplace were motionless, the smoke poised in clouds and billows all around the room.

Elizabeth whipped round. "Mother!" she cried. But Jane was frozen as well, her arms reaching for her daughter, her lips parted to summon her from the room. Elizabeth turned wildly to Isabella. "What's happened to her? What have you done?" she demanded.

Before Isabella could answer, the tribe of goblins began to melt. Their dark, barky bodies dissolved like so much ice turning into water. Swiftly the fluid matter streamed to-gether into one pool in the middle of the room. Then the pool rose up and up, taking the form of a tall man with long black hair and fierce golden eyes. His hands and feet were clawed, and he had wings of inky black feathers. Bands of dark gold were clasped around his wrists and neck, and great golden rings glinted on his fingers.

Elizabeth stared and her mind emptied. Worries about her family, Thomas Montford, Merrivale, Isabella—even the course of her own life—fell away, faded by the creature's glory.

The faerie turned, his eyes fixed on her. His lips were the dark red of blood dropped on snow, and he spoke words she couldn't understand. Something welled up inside of her . . . an ache, a longing. She felt as though she were being lifted from the narrow bounds of her life to see from a great height all the long ages of the earth: the birth of man, the rising up and falling away of gods, idols, dynasties, and kingdoms. She sensed the doors to another realm blow open, giving her a glimpse of an older, darker world that lay alongside her own. Nothing about her own small life mattered. Nothing.

"Elizabeth! Elizabeth, look at me!" Isabella clapped her hands in front of Elizabeth's face, and finally something seemed to snap shut inside of her. She stumbled forward, drawing a great gasp of air, filling her lungs.

"Come now," Isabella said. "I'll take you to a safe place."

Elizabeth looked around wildly. "What of Mother?" she said. "I can't leave her."

"We'll only be gone for a moment," Isabella said. "Come with me now."

"No!" Elizabeth cried. She turned away, reaching out to her mother. But before she could touch the frozen figure, the faerie scooped her up and put her and Isabella onto his back. A moment later they were in the air, clinging to the crow man as he returned to the hawthorn tree where Isabella had created a pathway into the shadow land.

Elizabeth closed her eyes tightly, as if she were trying to block out all she had seen in the last few moments. Isabella squeezed her friend's hand in sympathy. She remembered all too well how *she* had felt the first time she'd beheld one of the crow people.

They traveled fast and soon reached the hawthorn tree. Over the topmost branches, a sliver of light appeared, like a long tear in a piece of parchment. The faerie cried out and dived through the split into the shadow land, carrying with him the two mortal beings.

20

The Prison

A cold wind billowed across the sky, and Isabella sank deeper into the bird's silken feathers. Elizabeth's eyes were still closed, but her lips were moving, as though she were talking to someone Isabella couldn't see.

Isabella sighed. She felt a mixture of emotions upon returning to the shadow land. In many ways it was more a home to her than the ordinary world. She had lived here for so long, and its contrary, confusing ways were familiar. But she had never truly belonged, as her brother, John, had come to belong. She was a changeling, a foreigner, a guest. Yet she didn't belong in the ordinary world, either. She had no earthly family and nowhere to call home—the two things she longed for most. She had seen so many marvels in the shadow land. But she willingly would exchange all those visions for a mother to cuddle with and a father to make her laugh, for a home with a fire to sit by at night and meals to share with her own people, the ones she loved and who loved her. The ancient and eternal were altogether too much for one mortal girl. She wanted ordinary intimacy instead, and it had been so long, so very long, since she'd had anything like that.

The men had come to arrest her mother at the heel of the autumn, the last dark days of November 1241. They arrived at the cottage early in the morning, one on horseback and two others on foot. Ruth was sitting in her chair nursing John, and Isabella was crouched by the fire, stirring barley porridge for their breakfast. The men kicked open the door without preamble and marched into the cottage. The leader unrolled a piece of parchment and read out a series of charges, accusing Ruth of practicing witchcraft, laying on curses, taking part in a witches' sabbath, consorting with demons, and causing the deaths of numerous babies and children. The men seemed to fill the little cottage, and they were careless of it, kicking furniture aside, overturning the cauldron of porridge so the contents spilled, steaming, all over the floor. Their voices were loud and hard.

Isabella was horrified by the men's angry manner, their pent-up violence, and the way they swaggered when they knocked Ruth's pots of herbs from the shelves. This was a show of bravado. Perhaps the men were afraid of Ruth, believing she was a powerful witch. Perhaps they had talked themselves into believing it, to cover up any unease they felt at making the arrest. After all, they were part of a small community, and Ruth knew two of the three. One she had treated when his wrist was broken in a fight; the other had a wife who would have died if Ruth had not supervised the difficult birth of his twin sons. Now neither of them would look her in the eye. Instead, they set about wrecking the cottage.

Ruth was surprisingly calm. She stood up, kissed her son on the top of his head, and handed him to Isabella. Then she kissed Isabella, too.

"Don't be afraid," she said.

The leader tied Ruth's wrists with a piece of rope, and the men led her out of the cottage.

Isabella was sick with dread. She knew too well what happened to women accused of witchcraft. All that day she stayed with John in the cottage, waiting for word of her mother—or her mother's release. She didn't clean up the mess the men had made. She just sat and waited, consumed by fear, expecting the worst. When night fell, John cried and cried, and Isabella cried, too. What was happening to her mother? How could she help her?

On the second day, unable to wait any longer, she tied John to her back in a shawl and headed to Maumesbury. The day was bitterly cold, the sky laden with heavy clouds that intermittently wet her with veils of freezing rain. Isabella, who had been unable to eat since her mother was taken, felt dead inside, her heart a rock. John wailed and struggled, but she didn't have the energy to comfort him. Instead, head down, she trudged on through the mud and the evil weather to the town crouched on the hill.

As she walked through the streets, people turned away from her as if she were a leper. They crossed themselves or made the sign against the evil eye. Even those her mother had helped moved from her path. Isabella tried not to see them, tried not to hear what they said. But every sideways glance, every word, seemed to pierce her.

She went to the courthouse and pounded on the door,

demanding to see her mother. The rain hammered on her bare head as she waited. The icy drops trickled through her clothes. And on her back John howled and shivered.

A guard opened the door. He stared at her, all limp and bedraggled, and took a quick breath as though he was about to send her off. But something changed his mind. Perhaps he took pity on her, because he stepped back and let her in. He led her to a small room and unlocked the door. "You can see her for a few minutes," he said gruffly.

Ruth was sitting on a low wooden pallet with a mattress of straw. She looked up. Her face was drawn and tired, but her smile seemed to illuminate the miserable room.

"Thank you for letting her see me," she said to the guard.

Isabella stepped inside; the door was locked behind her, and the guard departed. For a moment, she just stared at her mother.

Ruth stood up. She untied the shawl and took John from Isabella's back. Immediately he went limp against her shoulder, falling deeply asleep. "How wet you are. How cold!" Ruth said, putting her free arm around Isabella and kissing her icy cheek.

Isabella didn't know what to say—couldn't speak—and she began to cry with huge, broken sobs. She was entirely overcome with fear and grief, and she was worn out from the day and night of waiting alone in the cottage. They sank down onto the pallet, the three of them, and Isabella cried herself into a daze.

The guard banged on the door, saying they had only a few minutes left.

Ruth sat up straight, stroked the tears from her daughter's face. "Listen to me," she said. "I've known what would happen, and I've prepared for it. There is no way out now. They will have what they want. And when I am gone, you won't be safe, either. They will come after you and John, too, Isabella. You must go to the shrine at the spring and open the doorway, as you have seen me do. When the faerie comes, tell him it's time for you to be taken. The crow people will give you a home in the shadow land. You will be safe with them."

Isabella drank in her mother's face. Wan as Ruth was, her eyes were bright with life, and she had never looked so beautiful. Isabella's heart seemed to collapse. "Don't leave me," she said. "Don't ask me to leave you."

"The faeries will take care of you. I have a bond with them. I secured a promise they won't break."

"Then why won't they save you? Why don't you hide in the shadow land, too?" Isabella pleaded. "Why have you given up?"

Ruth didn't take her eyes from her daughter's face. "The faerie who visits the shrine in the woods—do you remember him, Isabella? John is his son. Do you understand? He wants his child. He has longed for him since John was born, but I've kept him for myself. Now I will let him take John, and in exchange, he will care for you, too. He will offer safety and protection to one mortal, in order to have his son."

She stroked Isabella's hair. Then she went on. "I've enjoyed a good life. I had my husband, and I've watched you grow and cared for you, and I've had my son, too. Now it's your turn to live. I'm not afraid of death, Isabella. It is only the end of one kind of life. But you haven't had a chance to enjoy what this life has to offer, so the faerie's gift goes to you. Travel with him to the shadow land and remain until it's safe for you to return."

"I don't want to leave you," Isabella said stubbornly. "I *can't* leave you. I don't want to be alone."

"You won't be alone. You'll have John. And I will be with you. I'll be with you always."

But Isabella wouldn't have it, this surrender. "You *won't* be with me!" she cried. "Not in the way I want you to be. You won't care for me. You won't see me grow up. I won't be able to touch you or talk to you. Why don't you fight the charges against you? Why?"

"The people have made up their minds. How can I fight them?" Ruth said. For a moment her show of courage faltered. Her lips trembled. Then she went on. "Of course I'm afraid. I'm frightened of what they will do to me. But that will be over soon, and I'm not frightened of what comes after. Be brave, Isabella. You come from a long line of wise women who've guarded the shrine. I've taught you everything I know, and you are the best daughter a mother could ever ask for. Take care of John, and try to be strong."

There were voices outside the room; it seemed that the guard was arguing with someone. Then the door was unlocked. "You must leave at once," he told Isabella. Instead, she flung her arms around her mother's neck and wouldn't let go. The guard had to tear her away, and she kicked and flailed about with her fists as he carried her out.

"Mother! Mother! Mother!" she screamed, blind with grief, while the man cursed and swore. He dumped her in the street, and a moment later, John was unceremoniously set down beside her in the mud, like so much unwanted garbage.

For a long time Isabella remained where she was, in the street outside the courthouse. She was oblivious to the cold and rain, insensible to the people scurrying past, all averting their eyes. She felt as if the whole world were falling away. How could she go on? The future was a mountain that she hadn't the strength to climb. John alternately squirmed or cuddled against her. He was very pale now, and his eyes were swollen with tears. He sucked his hand hungrily, poked her face and tugged her hair. In the end his strength began to ebb, and he curled up, half on her lap and half on the street. Dimly, from a great distance, Isabella saw how cold and hungry he was and realized his life was in her hands. She picked him up and set off for home.

The rain had stopped, and darkness was falling as they left the town. To the west the clouds burned red and gold. In the east the moon rose, large and brilliant, like a jewel. But Isabella turned her eyes away from the sky and to the ground and trudged back to the broken cottage.

All night, while John slept on their mother's bed, Isabella sat up and gazed into space. Her mother had sacrificed herself in order that Isabella and John might escape, but this did not fill her with any sense of gratitude. Instead, she was eaten by guilt. If it weren't for Isabella, Ruth could have been the one mortal the crow people would accept. Ruth could have escaped into the shadow land to live with John and his father. It was Isabella who prevented it from happening. How could she know this and go on?

Isabella was not surprised that John's father was one of the crow people. Perhaps there was no space in her heart for surprise. Or perhaps she had known all along. John's black hair, the strange gold flecks in his eyes, pointed to his faerie origin. But he was delightfully human, too, with his fragrant, perfect-blossom skin, his hearty appetite, his cries and smiles.

Isabella felt implacable anger stir in her chest for the faerie who yearned for his son and cared so little for his son's mother that he would allow her to be executed. Why couldn't the faerie bend the rules? Why wouldn't he take them all and keep them safe? Isabella ground her teeth. The crow people didn't live by the same rules as mortals; that much she understood. They had no sense of morality or obligation. Their promises were like reflections on the surface of a pond—impossible to grasp. Yet somehow her mother had wrested one from them. How had she done it? What powers had it taken to make such a bargain?

All the long night, Isabella ran over and over the same thoughts, trying in vain to make sense of things. Her memories were sharp knives. Even the cottage in which she had spent so many happy years seemed hostile, the table thrown over, the precious chair broken, the floor awash with spilled herbs and broken crockery.

Slowly the moon passed overhead, the great, white face shining down upon the rooftop. By dawn Isabella's grief had drained away, leaving behind only an icy, empty space. She blotted out the last painful memory of her mother's face, unable to bear the thought of the humiliating trial and the cruel, inevitable execution that would follow. Only John existed for her now, and she had to keep going for his sake. When her brother—her *half* brother—woke up, she left the cottage and took him to the shrine in the forest.

21

The Shadow Land

lizabeth dreamed she was falling. She was warm and comfortable, and the feeling of falling was familiar. She had dreamed it before, and she was close enough to waking to be drowsily confident she wouldn't hit the ground. She was safe from harm, feeling the heat of her sister's body beside her. Her parents lay together in the other bedroom . . . her brother would return from Oxford soon . . . and they would all be together. She had nothing to worry about anymore.

The ground rose like a huge, soft hand and cradled her. A mound of blankets covered her. She turned on her side, ready to yield to deep, delicious sleep. All was well. She wanted nothing to disturb her now.

"Elizabeth! Elizabeth!"

Like the buzz of an irritant fly, a voice broke into her dreaming. She tried to ignore it.

"Elizabeth!" the voice persisted—and someone was shaking her now. It had to be Esther.

"Go away," she said. "Leave me alone."

"Wake up. You must wake up."

The voice needled into Elizabeth's ears and mind. Reluctantly she opened her eyes and tried to sit up. Bright light
dazzled. This wasn't her bedroom! Where was she? All she
could see was brilliant white—except in front of her, a green
girl was squatting and staring at her anxiously.

"Are you awake now? Are you well?" the green girl said.
She moved from side to side, still squatting, as though she
were trying to peer right through Elizabeth's eyes and into
her head.

Elizabeth squinted, trying to make sense of her sur-
roundings. She wasn't covered in blankets. She was lying in
a deep bed of snow, though strangely she wasn't at all cold.
She realized she must still be dreaming—one didn't feel cold
in dreams. The landscape was obliterated with snow, a vast
plain spreading under a vivid blue sky. Very far away, mountains rose, blue with distance. She stared at the green girl,
who was hopping up and down now, very like a little frog.
The girl seemed anxious, and Elizabeth wanted to reassure
her. *Everything is fine,* she thought. *No need to worry. It's just a
dream.*

"Elizabeth, it isn't a dream," the green girl said in a loud
and startling voice, as though she had heard Elizabeth's
thoughts. "You've got to wake up properly. We haven't got
long. We have to move."

When Elizabeth still didn't respond, the green girl
clasped her face and whispered two words into her ear: "Kit
Merrivale."

Elizabeth shook her head. A storm of thoughts and
impressions swirled through her mind. *Merrivale.* The name
resounded like a gong, and everything fell into place: her

imprisonment, her mother, the goblins crawling over the house, the faerie with eyes of gold—and the knife flying toward Isabella. The knife!

She gulped for breath, the shock of remembering like a splash of cold water on her face. "Isabella!" she cried, her voice choked. "You . . . you're . . . I saw the knife. I thought you'd be killed!"

Isabella stepped back. "As you see, I'm not dead."

Elizabeth looked around in wonder. "Where are we? Is this . . . is this the shadow land?"

Isabella nodded.

Elizabeth was trembling now. In some way she hadn't truly believed in the shadow land until the faerie assembled himself from his goblin parts and reared up before her. It was one thing to hear stories of elves and faeries and monsters, to imagine them hidden in the darkness. It was another to find the real, predictable world tugged out from under your feet. She felt she was walking on thin ice that might break at any moment. She had no idea what would happen, what to expect.

Even Isabella looked unfamiliar. Elizabeth stared at her friend. In the mortal world she had appeared outlandish, with her green skin, claw nails, and hair like a wolf's pelt. But here in the shadow land Isabella seemed inexplicably larger and brighter. Here she glowed as green as an emerald. Her face was beautiful and luminous; her eyes shone; her hair hung to her waist, a silky forest green. Sunlight glinted off jewels set in a coronet on her head—except there *was* no coronet, in reality. It flickered in and out of sight.

"You look . . . I can't explain it, but you look different,"

Elizabeth said. She tried to understand it, to pinpoint the change. It was as though she was seeing Isabella's vital, essential self—her immortal soul—with all the ordinariness, all the muddy clutter of mortal life washed away.

"You, also," Isabella said quietly. "You're different, too. It's this place."

Elizabeth stood up. She breathed deeply, drawing in the keen air. And she laughed, her fears receding. Her mood had changed completely, and the newness of the shadow land seemed exhilarating instead of terrifying. She turned to Isabella. "I'm ready," she said. "What happens now?" She gestured to the snowy plains. "It looks as though we're miles and miles from anywhere. How far will we have to walk?"

Isabella took her hand. "Not so far," she said.

They set off toward the distant mountains. The snow was beautiful and soft, a powder of glittering crystals. The two girls broke the smooth, endless surface with their feet, but looking behind them, Elizabeth saw the snow scurry over the marks they had left, making their footprints vanish.

She was excited now, and full of questions. "Where did the faerie go? The one who brought us here? And what about my mum? Is she still in the house with Kit Merrivale?" Worry rose as she thought about her mother. Just like her feeling of exhilaration a moment before, this feeling was overwhelming—and it was reflected in the landscape. The mountains, the plains of snow, even the vanishing footprints began to seem ominous and hostile. What had she been thinking? She and Isabella were helpless and alone. They would die out here, with no one to hear them calling for help. Elizabeth stopped walking, paralyzed by panic. She couldn't breathe, and she shut her eyes, desperate to escape.

"Your mother is safe for now. Don't be afraid. Open your eyes." Isabella squeezed her hand. "Try not to worry," she said. "What you're feeling changes everything. Let your fear go. Let it go, or we won't get anywhere."

Elizabeth opened her eyes.

"Keep walking," Isabella went on. "Come. I'll talk as we go. We haven't got much time, you see." Her voice was very clear and calm, and she sounded like an adult talking to a child—gently cajoling and encouraging, trying to inspire confidence.

She's lived here for centuries, Elizabeth reminded herself. *She knows what to do. Trust her.* She nodded and began to walk again.

"The faerie who brought us here is a crow prince and my brother's father," Isabella said. "He loved my mother—as much as any faerie can love a woman from the shadow land. That's what they call *our* world, you see. We think the shadow land is a reflection of our world, and they think our world is a reflection of theirs. Because we live and fail and die and they live forever, our world seems a very pitiful place— a crudely formed lower world. Except that it seems to attract them, too. They can't leave us alone. Despite their disdain, they keep coming back. I've learned a great deal about the crow people, but I don't entirely understand what it is about us that they need and desire. But there's something . . . some connection between us."

Elizabeth nodded. "Where is your mother now—and your brother?" she asked.

"My mother was a midwife and a healer. She was falsely

accused of heresy and witchcraft, and she was executed," Isabella said in a small, tight voice.

Elizabeth gasped, too shocked to speak. She clutched her friend's arm.

"Mother . . . Mother managed to save me and John by making a pact with the Faerie Queen—John's grandmother," Isabella went on. "The queen wanted John so much, so passionately, that she agreed to take care of me if she could have him. It's hard to understand how faeries think, but maybe she didn't like my mother—or at least she didn't like her son loving a woman made of dirt. That's what they think of us, you see. That we're made of dirt."

"That's what it says in the Bible," Elizabeth murmured. "'For dust you are, and unto dust you shall return.'"

Isabella gazed at the distant mountains for a moment. "I have been in the shadow land for years and years. In some ways it doesn't seem so long; in other ways it seems forever. It's always like that here. Not days and nights lined up, one after another. A few times I went back to the mortal world. I met Jerome, the hermit who lived by the spring, and he became my friend. We learned a lot from each other. He knew who I truly was. But I never felt safe, and I didn't want to be parted from my brother, so I came back here again. The faeries have allowed me to stay, and the crow prince has sometimes helped me for my mother's sake. But they have never cared for me very much because I'm not one of them. Not like my brother."

Isabella gave Elizabeth a small smile. "My brother, John, is faerie royalty—a prince and a warrior," she said. "The shadow land is all he can remember, and he is more faerie than human now. Still, he was all I had—until I met you. I can't quite explain it, but I knew when we met that you would be my friend and you would help me find a place in the world again."

Elizabeth nodded. Her friend's trust and faith weighed heavily, but they were precious gifts, too. "I will do everything I can," she said, putting her hand to her heart. "Yet it seems I've just caused you more trouble. You've gotten caught up in accusations of heresy again—except that this time it's *my* mother who is in danger."

"I couldn't help my mother. I *didn't* help her," Isabella said sadly. "She made the choice to sacrifice herself for me, but I've always felt guilty. Perhaps if I can help you save your mother, some of the debt I made for myself will be paid."

"What's happening to my mother and Merrivale and the men in the house?" Elizabeth asked. "What's happening now?"

"Nothing. They're still there . . . and *we're* still there, too," said Isabella. "The faerie just pulled us away for one moment. When we go back, we'll return to the same moment."

Elizabeth frowned. "I don't understand."

"Imagine that time is a long, long piece of string," said Isabella. "Imagine that when the faerie took us away from the house, he tied a knot in the string, making a loop that lies alongside it. We're in that loop. We have an extra piece of time outside the regular flow. But it's not a very big piece, and when we go back, it will be to the knot where we started out. Do you see?"

"I think so," Elizabeth said slowly. On one level what

Isabella was telling her made sense. On another it was non-sense! How could time be tied in knots? Then again, how could she be here? She would just have to accept what Isabella was saying. She would have to trust that her mother was safe for the time being. There was nothing else she could do.

Isabella was silent for a while. Her long grass-green hair rose and fell, even though the air was still. Sunlight glinted on the coronet that appeared and disappeared again from her head. "I think there is a way I can save your mother," she said at last. "I understand the shadow world much better now than when I lost mine. I know so much more—even more than *she* knew, because she never crossed over to this side. She was clever and wily in dealing with the faeries, and I can be, too. I will find the Faerie Queen, and we shall come to an agreement."

For a moment Elizabeth was a little afraid of her friend, because Isabella did not look like a girl any longer—even a magical green girl. When she spoke of cunning and wiles, her eyes were old. All three hundred years of her life were there: the weight of her mother's horrible fate, the fear of persecution, the centuries of trying to make a place for herself among the terrible, beautiful crow people. Then Isabella smiled, and the moment passed. She was Elizabeth's friend once again—shy and vulnerable, generous and kind, with an inner strength that soothed and comforted.

"Where does the queen live?" Elizabeth asked. "How will we find her?"

"Under a shadow, between the stars . . . turn right at mid-night and walk until dawn," Isabella answered with a grin.

"There isn't a known way. Perhaps she's everywhere. But don't worry, we'll find her." Isabella pointed. "Look ahead."

Elizabeth raised her face. Without her even noticing, they had reached the once-distant mountains. She shaded her eyes. In the same way she kept seeing Isabella's coronet of jewels flash in and out of existence, she now saw a mighty city superimposed upon the bleak, perilous mountains. There were palaces of gray stone, slender towers with onion domes glittering like pearls, terraces in the clouds, steep roads, and bridges with countless arches poised over tumbling rivers.

Elizabeth shuddered. Despite its magnificence, the city looked as cold and dangerous as the mountains. Isabella had said there wasn't a known way to reach it, but the unknown path had brought them here, and Elizabeth was afraid to go any farther.

22

Jerome

After two long days underground, Thomas Montford felt the weight of the silence. The floating orb gave light enough, he had water to drink from the spring, and by the end of the second day the pangs of hunger had died away. Yet the silence troubled him. So from time to time, simply to create a noise, to please himself with the sound, he rattled a string of rosary beads inside the golden chalice he'd found the first day.

It was hard to gauge time accurately, but his body seemed to know when to sleep and when to wake, and this had happened twice. On rising each time, he returned to the chapel with the wall paintings, knelt, and prayed before the shining monstrance. Then he drank and washed at the spring before returning to the abbey's secret library to read.

It was the opportunity of a lifetime to browse among these shelves. The collection was beyond value—a testimony to the accomplishments of the most learned monks in what had been one of the most powerful monasteries in Europe. There were books of poetry, history, and law. There were books that chronicled the lives of saints, and books of obscure philosophy. There were ancient maps rolled up and sealed with wax. Thomas felt privileged to be in the library, but he also worried about how he would get out. Only Elizabeth knew exactly where he was and how to open the door. If she had been captured or arrested or was simply unable to get back to the church, might he not starve to death? He struggled to put these fears behind him. God had protected him so far. He must trust in the Lord to preserve him now.

Thomas was fascinated by the books of science and magic, though most of them exceeded his understanding. He longed to know how the floating light was fashioned and why it produced no heat. Most often, however, he turned to the writings of Saint Jerome, the hermit of the woods who was blessed with visions of angels and had painted them upon the chapel wall. Thomas wanted to know why Jerome had painted a green girl among them.

At the end of the second day, he found what he was looking for. In a long, ecstatic piece of writing, Jerome described how a column of angels with wings of black feathers had descended upon the forest at the Virgin Mary's shrine. He wrote how beautiful they were, how he fell to his knees in worship. And how they had left behind a little girl for him to care for— a green girl whose name was Isabella Leland. She was a child, Jerome wrote, of quiet strength and great wisdom, who taught him the properties of healing herbs and explained to him much about the nature of angels. She also told him that her mother had entrusted her and her brother to the angels after being accused of practicing witchcraft.

Thomas faltered in his reading. Witchcraft? How had this come about? Surely the woman must have been innocent if she could call upon angels to take care of her children.

He read on, burning with curiosity.

They were friends, the hermit and the angels' child, for several months. The girl lived wild in the forest, for she still was in terror of persecution and witch hunters. Then one day an angel returned to claim Isabella, and she disappeared. Jerome returned to the abbey for a time and described his visions to his fellow members of the secret inner order. The visitations were considered too strange and dangerous for the ordinary abbey monks to know about, but Jerome was invited to re-create his angels on the walls of the underground chapel.

Jerome also examined the court records for the previous century and found the notes taken during the trial of one Ruth Leland.

"She was tried by the civil authorities, not the church, after a wealthy and powerful local family made a charge against her because a baby had died," Jerome had written. "In fact, it appears that the church authorities tried to protect her because they respected her learning and knew she had spoken with angels at the Virgin's shrine, as I have done. One Matthias Dyer, an abbey servant, spoke in her defense at the trial and poured scorn on the superstitions of the ignorant. But the accused woman would not reveal the name of the father of her second child, a son called John. Her adamant refusal went against her, and the malice of the bereaved family knew no bounds. Despite the testimony provided by the abbey, the judge found her guilty. She was sentenced to be hanged by the neck until she was dead."

The priest was stunned. His first feeling was an overwhelming pity for Isabella and her mother. His second was amazement at the bond between the two families, made so long ago. How much did Elizabeth know of this? One of her forefathers had tried to defend Ruth Leland. It was an extraordinary tale.

Jerome wrote little else about his green visitor. He saw Isabella only one more time. This was when he was an elderly man, and life in the cold cell at the shrine was becoming an increasing struggle. Isabella returned to him alone—still the child he remembered. For despite the years that had passed, she had not grown older. She had in her arms a bundle of dry old bones that she begged him to keep secret and safe. She told him to whom the bones belonged—but not why they should be treasured. Even so, Jerome had honored her request. He carried the bones to the abbey and secured them in the secret chapel.

Thomas closed the book. In the silence of the library, he could hear the beating of his heart and a curious singing in his ears. Isabella had lived with the angels. It was hard to believe. He had seen her . . . spoken to her . . . smelled her perfume of cold woods, leaves, and dirt. She had seemed so flesh-and-blood to him. But she had helped him, hadn't she? And more than once. Probably, he owed her his life. It couldn't be chance that she had returned at this time—first warning him about Merrivale's arrival, then taking him to the spring in the woods, and later helping Elizabeth guide him to the hidden place beneath the hill.

Thomas crossed himself and offered prayers of thanks. His fever of excitement burned again. He had placed his fate in the hands of God, and God had sent a child to protect him.

23

The Faerie Queen

sabella and Elizabeth stood before the huge silver gates leading into the great stone city. Isabella knew how hard this was on her friend, how afraid and confused she must feel. But at least Elizabeth had a guide to help her. Isabella hadn't had anyone to show her the way when she had first come to the shadow land. The Faerie Queen had taken John from her, and Isabella had been left to fend for herself in the palace.

Elizabeth blinked and rubbed her eyes.

"What do you see?" Isabella asked.

"It changes. Mountains—and a grove of birch trees. And then it shifts, and I see a huge city and a shining silver gate. Which is true, Isabella?"

"They're both true. The shadow land has many layers, and they shift, so you have to fix your thoughts on the one you're looking for. Right now it is the city we want. At the heart of it we'll find the queen's palace. But the city will be difficult. Wishing for it will take us the right way, but the queen needs to wish it, too. Or at least she must not wish us *not* to find her."

"I don't understand," said Elizabeth. Her gaze went flat for a moment, as if she were looking at something far away that Isabella couldn't see. Then she came back again and smiled at her friend. "I'll follow you," she said. "I trust you. How do we open the gates?"

"We walk through the birch trees. It is useful that we can do that. The faeries can't, you see. They get caught up in one particular story, and then they have to follow it to the end. We can wriggle in between them."

Elizabeth looked at her sideways. "You had to learn so much, living here," she said. "It must have been difficult."

"Like being a mouse," Isabella whispered. "You can't feed at the table, so you learn how to scuttle along the floorboards and steal the crumbs. You find secret ways around the house that only you are small enough to use. That's what we are, Elizabeth. Mice. Can you do it? Look for the birch trees and fix on them."

"Hold my hand so we can pass through together," Elizabeth said. "I don't want to be caught on one side of the gate with you on the other."

They stared at the silver gates, and Isabella summoned up in her mind the image of the great mountains that lay beneath the spectacle of the faerie city. The towers and mansions and roads receded, the gate began to melt, and its bars became the slender trunks of the birch trees. She took her friend's hand, and they stepped through.

A great noise filled the air behind them, and Elizabeth whipped around. The silver gates had reappeared, and they were standing inside the stone city. Outside, the snow had vanished, and a clamor arose from the plains—the clash of swords, the fierce cries of warriors, the screams of the wounded. Long banners of scarlet and gold floated above the ranks of two great armies. The scent of smoke and blood drifted from the battle.

"Why are they fighting? What is happening?" Elizabeth asked, clutching Isabella's arm.

"Look away. Come with me," Isabella said. "The battle goes on and on forever." She pulled Elizabeth from the gates, but her friend kept looking back, overawed by the spectacle.

The city loomed all around them now. Tall houses flanked the stone road. Occasionally the road opened into a square with a fountain and flowers. The architecture was beautiful and strange—even nonsensical. Doors were not necessarily on the ground. Many were set on the first or second floor, so that anyone stepping out would tumble to the earth. Some of the buildings had no windows at all, while others had windows that revealed not the interior of a house but views of forests and deserts—or vistas of other cities. Towers sprouted here and there, but defying logic, they leaned or floated above the ground. The sky continually changed, as though days and nights were racing above their heads. Clouds hurtled and boiled, the storms followed by intervals of burning sunshine. The city was a cauldron of images. And it was deserted.

Elizabeth still held Isabella's hand. "I don't like it here. It frightens me," she said. "Where are the crow people?"

"They're here," Isabella said. "We just aren't seeing them at the moment. Don't be afraid. They won't hurt us." But she was nervous, too. With the notable exception of her brother, John, she had never brought anyone to the shadow land before. She didn't think the crow people would hurt her and Elizabeth, but they might play some cruel tricks on them.

The girls plodded on through the maze of streets. Isabella sighed. For so long she had skulked around the faerie court, snatching every moment she could to be in John's company. It had been very painful to see how swiftly he had embraced his faerie heritage and become one of them.

After Isabella brought John to the shadow land, he had been tended by a faerie nurse, who—for her role in this tale of the changeling son—took on the appearance of a bent old crow woman with gray feathers and an ugly beaked face. The boy slept in a golden cradle, his clothes were adorned with pearls, and every day he was taken to the Faerie Queen to be cuddled and doted upon. He was given a new name; in the language of the crow people he was called Beloved of the Queen. But he didn't stay a child as Isabella, the girl made of dirt, did. He became a prince of the shadow land, and he all but forgot about his sister.

But Isabella had never forgotten about him. She still loved him, the only remaining family she had. She traveled throughout the realm of the faeries, but she always returned, to hide in her mouse holes, to catch a glimpse of her brother.

"What did you mean about the faeries getting caught up in stories?" Elizabeth asked. "Tell me more about them. What are they like?"

"It's hard to understand," Isabella replied. "The crow people don't live like us, in straight lines with every day new and unknown. Their lives are long, long stories that are told again and again, reenacted over and over. Some I've seen for myself, like the battle outside the gates. Others my mother told me. There's a story of a princess who is cursed and locked up in a palace to sleep for a hundred years until a prince breaks the enchantment. And there's a story about a girl who wanders through a forest and gets torn apart by wolves. One of the she-wolves gives birth to her in wolf form, and the girl becomes queen of the pack. There are so many tales . . . more than I will ever know . . . and they aren't exactly the same each time. Over the centuries they alter bit by bit and find new shapes.

"The faeries also eat and sleep and argue and play," Isabella went on. "And sometimes they cross over to our world. But it is stories that make the shape of a faerie's immortal life. I think that's why the Faerie Queen loves John so much. He is a fresh beginning . . . a new story . . . and he makes the old stories new as well."

Elizabeth was quiet a moment, as if trying to make sense of Isabella's words. Then she looked around. "We've been walking for hours," she said. "Everything looks the same, and I'm getting tired. How much farther is it?"

Isabella sighed. "I don't know. Be patient. Think about the palace. Think about being there."

Elizabeth stopped short. "Why did you say that?" she cried. "How can you say such a thing?"

Isabella also halted. "What?" she said.

Elizabeth jammed her hands to her head, blocking her ears. "No! No! Don't say that!" She looked at Isabella, and her eyes widened. She backed away. Then she made the sign of the cross.

"What is it? What are you seeing?" Isabella demanded. "Look at me! I'm your friend Isabella."

Elizabeth seemed to hear other words entirely, because she moaned and crossed herself again, and she backed away as Isabella stepped closer.

Isabella's mind raced. What was happening? What trickery was this? How could she make Elizabeth see the truth?

Elizabeth clutched her hands together and surveyed the faerie city. The walls faded, and inside the houses she could see ghostly figures. They acted out their daily tasks—lighting cooking fires, grinding wheat, baking, sewing—but, sensing Elizabeth, they looked up and stared with empty eyes from hollow faces. Their hands were worn to the bone, and their clothes were rags. Their voices echoed in Elizabeth's mind.

Beware. Do not trust her, the voices said. *Do not follow her, or you will be trapped as we are. Turn back. Leave before it is too late.*

"No," Elizabeth moaned. "No, it can't be. It can't be!"

The voices spoke of suffering and despair. Was this a circle of hell? The place of no hope? A current of pain and grief swirled around Elizabeth, summoning images of long nights alone in the cold, of a hunger that would never be satisfied, of grief beyond the reach of comfort. She saw her father in Venice, holding his face in his hands . . . her sister, Esther, weeping in the house in Maumesbury, the housekeeper long gone. And there was Robert, being tortured to reveal his secrets . . . and her mother, her hair turned white and her wits lost from having been locked up for years. Elizabeth had failed them all.

She glanced at Isabella, and her heart seemed to freeze. The beautiful green girl had disappeared. Now Elizabeth saw a hideous goblin lady—Isabella's height, but worn and decayed like a corpse. The skin that stretched over her face was as dry as paper. Her lips pulled back over black and broken teeth. Her hands were torn, the skin in rags, though great, glittering rings shone on her fingers.

How can anyone live for three hundred years? the voices whispered. *This is what she truly looks like. Clear your eyes. Don't follow her any farther, Elizabeth.*

Isabella laughed. "Now I have you," she said. "Your immortal soul belongs to me. And there is no use in calling on God, because he won't hear you. There is nothing you can do."

Suddenly, Elizabeth didn't feel frightened anymore. She hadn't the energy for it. Instead, despair seeped through the alleyways of her mind and filled the bright spaces of her thoughts and memories. Slowly she turned from Isabella and wandered back through the city. This way the road was easier, leading her downhill.

Left behind, the Isabella goblin jumped up and down, cursing and uttering blasphemies, but Elizabeth didn't care anymore. All she had treasured was lost. All joy had been sucked from her life. The future was an abyss of loneliness, suffering, and decline.

One of the somber ghosts stepped out into the road and beckoned her to follow it into a house. Elizabeth passed across the threshold into a dim little room. The ghost nodded and gestured to a low stone couch by the wall. Elizabeth lay down, her knees curled to her chest. The couch was hard and cold as ice.

Isabella tried to work out what her friend was seeing. She knew the crow people were all around them, even though they remained invisible. What were they saying to Eliza-beth? She seemed to think Isabella was evil—and to hear something entirely different from what Isabella was actually saying. Elizabeth's eyes glazed over, and her shoulders sagged as if her courage and spirit had ebbed away. She turned and trudged down the stone road.

"Elizabeth!" Isabella called. "Listen to me. The faeries are toying with you. Believe in me! Please!" But Elizabeth paid no attention. She stepped off the stone road into one of the grand houses and disappeared from view.

Isabella didn't know what to do. It was a cruel faerie trick, to split them up. Should she leave Elizabeth to fend for herself and set off alone in pursuit of the queen? Or should she follow Elizabeth? She hopped from one foot to another, unable to decide. The faeries were powerful. If they really wanted to keep Elizabeth, there was little Isabella could do about it. But how afraid her friend must be, lost and alone, trapped in a very bad dream. She had to help her.

Isabella ran to the house that had swallowed Elizabeth, but the walls had sealed themselves against her. She slammed her fist against one of them in frustration. "Let me in!" she shouted. "Let me in!" Far away she heard music and laughter. The sound rippled along the road like a ribbon. Then, like a woman adjusting her skirts, the house shifted on its foundations, its walls folding and creasing. It shrank, and in a heartbeat it was a box small enough for Isabella to hold in her hand.

"No!" she shouted. "No, that's not fair!" The ribbon of laughter drifted past her again and then was gone. Isabella choked back tears. It was too hard. How could she fight them when they shaped reality? "I hate you," she whispered. "For what you did and for what you didn't do. I hate you."

She bent down and picked up the house. The whole city was shifting now. The towers, mansions, and market squares became insubstantial. The colors faded to a succession of grays, and then the city disappeared entirely. Isabella was left in a rocky wilderness, a plain of broken granite interspersed with a few bare and stunted trees.

The wind howled. Isabella opened her fingers. The tiny house was now a simple piece of rough stone. The wasteland stretched around her, as far as the eye could see. In all her long years in the shadow land, she had never felt so utterly alone. She had lost her mother. She had lost her brother. She had lost her friend. There was no one in the ordinary world or in the shadow land whom she could call on for help. She crouched down, clutching the stone to her chest.

Isabella spent many years in the wasteland, growing ragged and mad. She had no one to talk to except the friend she imagined lived in a piece of stone that she always carried around. She eked out an existence eating roots and leaves. The sky was always gray with clouds, and sometimes the rain poured down. She huddled against the rocks in narrow ravines to protect herself from the weather. From time to time she would see a flock of birds flying overhead, and once, far away on the horizon, she saw a knight ride past on a black horse. She called out to him, but the knight was caught up in his own story and didn't respond. Finally, words deserted her and she lived like an animal, without a voice in her head. She forgot her own name.

Bleak days and nights followed; empty years, storms and rain.

"Isabella. Isabella."

Isabella stirred in her sleep. The voice sent thrills down her spine and seemed to touch the deepest places in her heart and mind.

"Isabella, wake up now. Wake up."

Isabella turned over. It was hard to wake up. She'd been asleep a long, long time. Her memories were jumbled.

"Sleepyhead," the voice admonished gently. "There's much to do. Come along."

Isabella's eyes flicked open, and she gasped. Swags of blossom nodded in the trees overhead. The air was sweet with the scent of apple and apricot. She was lying in an orchard on soft, lush grass embroidered with spring flowers. And beside her, stroking her hair, was her mother. Ruth was pretty, as she had been before their troubles began. Her face was fresh and bright.

For a moment, Isabella couldn't breathe. She was overcome. Memories tumbled over themselves in her mind—the long years in the wasteland, John, Elizabeth, Kit Merrivale, Thomas Montford.

"I told you that I would be with you," Ruth said. "You didn't believe me then, but it was true."

Isabella struggled to speak. "Is this another trick? Is it really you?" It was agony to doubt her mother, but it would be worse to believe her—and then find that Ruth's face was a mask for the Faerie Queen.

"It is," Ruth said gravely. "I've come to help you, but I haven't much time."

"Where are we?" Isabella said.

"We're on the edge of the shadow land," Ruth replied. "The ordinary world and the shadow land are like two sides of one coin—inseparable. But however large they appear, however much they seem like the beginning and end, they are but one single pebble on the beach of creation. There are many worlds beyond the two you know. Your journey has just begun. I'm one step ahead of you, that's all."

A breeze passed through the trees, stirring the blossoms, and Ruth looked over her shoulder. "The Faerie Queen senses my presence," she said. "I have to go soon. This is what you need—to help you see a clear way." She held out a small mirror, shining like a silver pool of water in her palm.

"Don't go. Please don't leave me alone again," Isabella begged. She embraced her mother, holding her tight.

"We'll be together again one day, I promise," Ruth whispered. "Don't forget what I said. I'm just one step ahead of you."

She got up and began to walk from the meadow. The breeze picked up, scattering blossoms from the trees. Very quickly, she became distant and insubstantial, blurring into the pale sky. Isabella strained her eyes to see, to make her out, but Ruth had disappeared.

The mirror lay on the grass. For a moment, the image of Ruth's face seemed to pass across its surface. Then it reflected only blossoms and sky. Slowly, Isabella reached out a hand and picked it up. In her other hand she still held the stone from the city. Her memories had all returned, and she felt her mother's presence, comforting her and giving her strength and determination.

The games were over, the battle had begun. "The stone city," she called, fixing it in her mind. "The stone city!"

Elizabeth stared at her own face. It was disconcerting. How could she be looking at herself?

"Elizabeth? It's me, Isabella. Can you hear what I'm saying?"

"Of course I can hear you." Elizabeth rubbed her eyes. Isabella was holding a small mirror in front of her face.

"Look in the mirror," Isabella urged. "Can you see what is real?"

"Where am I?" Elizabeth sat up and gazed about her. They appeared to be in a cold living room with a bare hearth and a distinct lack of adornments. She had been lying on a very hard and uncomfortable stone couch.

"Look at me," Isabella demanded.

Elizabeth was puzzled. "I *am* looking at you."

"And you can see me—as I am?"

"Of course! What do you mean?" Elizabeth felt a little irritable, as though she had woken too quickly. "I had a terrible dream," she said, struggling to remember. "I can't think what it was about, but it was frightening and sad."

Isabella nodded. "The faeries made stories of the fears and doubts we each carried, and we were lost," she said. "But now we will make our own story. Come. The queen's palace is very close. We will find her now."

Elizabeth smiled. "Show me where we must go."

When they stepped outside, it was nighttime. The city was bright with moonlight, and at the top of the road, clearly visible, stood the palace of the Faerie Queen. It was a forest of archways, towers, and domes, and it glimmered like a pearl in the silvery light. Elizabeth followed Isabella through the open gates and across the white-paved courtyard to the huge arched doors that opened to admit them.

They ran along corridors of marble inlaid with precious stones that seemed to provide the palace with magical illumination. Unerringly, Isabella led them up a great stairway to a pair of tall golden doors carved with leaves and grapes.

"This is the great hall—the Faerie Queen's throne room," Isabella said.

"Why hasn't anyone stopped us? Does she know we're here?" Elizabeth asked.

"Of course she does," Isabella replied. "Now we have to ask her to help us."

The golden doors opened, and the two girls stood together on the threshold of the room. It was vast. Walls lined with arched windows receded into the distance. Tiles of white and silver paved the floor. Isabella took Elizabeth's hand, and they entered together.

At the end of the long, long room, on a throne on a dais, sat the Faerie Queen. Her court was gathered all around her—tall men and women with long black hair and cloaks of inky feathers. Their bodies were adorned with heavy belts, bracelets, and necklaces. They wore rings in their ears and on their long white fingers.

Elizabeth trembled as the faeries turned their beautiful, fierce faces to see who had dared enter the queen's throne room. Perhaps she would have faltered if Isabella hadn't held her hand so tightly. But step by step the two girls crossed the tiled floor.

A tall man was seated at the queen's right hand. He looked like the others—except that his eyes were a warm brown flecked with gold, whereas the faeries' were cold yellow.

He must be John, Elizabeth thought. *He is Isabella's brother.*

When they reached the dais, Isabella dropped to her knees and pulled Elizabeth down beside her. A murmur rose among the assembly like a gust of wind and died away to a perfect silence.

Elizabeth lifted her face and regarded the queen of the faeries. Of all the crow people she was the palest. Her skin was white as snow, and her slanted eyes shone an antique gold. Two locks of her hair were plaited with beads of pearl and amber. The rest was loose and fell in thick coils to her feet. She wore a crown the color of iron in which a single white gem shone like the moon. Elizabeth looked away. It was difficult to gaze upon the queen for long . . . like trying to look at the sun.

"I am the first and the eldest of the crow people," the queen said. "What you call the shadow land sprang from me. These are all my children and grandchildren." She raised her hand and gestured to the court. "You, girl of dirt, wish to claim Beloved of the Queen, the one who is most precious to me."

Elizabeth shivered. The queen's voice was as chilly as the deepest, darkest days of winter.

Isabella rose to her feet. "I wish to make a contract with you, as my mother did before me," she said. "I have a claim on John because he is my brother . . . my flesh and blood . . . but I am prepared to relinquish my claim, provided you help me."

Elizabeth shook her head in confusion. What did Isabella mean? Was she truly prepared to give up her brother?

The Faerie Queen's eyes were fixed on Isabella, and Elizabeth saw the faintest tremor of emotion cross her regal face.

"The crow people have fierce loyalties and burning desires, but they do not love in the way that humans do," she whispered. "Love is an emotion unique to the people made of dirt. John is one of you as well as one of us. He feels love—and this woke something inside of me." The queen pressed her fist to her chest, her face compressed in pain.

"I loved him from the moment he was born, but your mother denied him to me for two long years. Can you understand what agony that was for me? Time for us isn't as it is for you. Two years seemed an eternity. That's why I wouldn't protect her when she came to me for help. I was angry. I took you, but I wouldn't raise a hand to protect your mother."

Elizabeth stood then and wrapped an arm around Isabella's waist, wanting to offer comfort. But Isabella didn't falter. She didn't take her eyes from the queen's face.

"Tell me what you want," the queen said.

"This is my friend, Elizabeth." Isabella said. "It is a small thing I ask, but it is important to her. Her family is in danger, and I want you to help them and keep them safe. In return, I will burn John's bones, hidden now in the ordinary world, and he will be free to stay here forever."

The queen turned to John. "Is this what you wish?" she asked.

John approached his sister. He dropped to his knees and took her in his arms. "Isabella, my sister, I don't remember you," he said. He pulled back, and his eyes, with their strange flecks of gold, searched her face. "You are my flesh and blood. But these are my people, Isabella. This is my home."

Isabella's eyes filled with tears. She threw her arms around her brother and held him tight.

How long did the embrace last? Elizabeth did not know. Days and nights and weeks and years? It lasted forever—and it lasted only a moment. Then Isabella loosed her grip and stepped back, and Beloved of the Queen, once her brother, John, returned to his grandmother.

The queen placed her long, bejeweled hand over his. "The contract is made," she said.

Reliquary

homas Montford was lightheaded from not eating. The candles in the chapel burned brightly, and the gold leaf on the wall painting glittered. Thomas made the sign of the cross, and his eyes filled with tears. He had seen so much, and his heart was full of gratitude and the love of God. How unworthy he was, and yet how blessed. Soon he would have to leave the hidden rooms, for surely Elizabeth wouldn't leave him to starve— she would find a way to help him escape Maumesbury. But he would carry with him forever the knowledge and experiences he had gained here.

Thomas held the jeweled rosary beads between his fingers. He found it hard to concentrate. Although he tried to steer his mind toward prayer, he wondered instead what had happened to Elizabeth and her family, and he mulled over the remarkable story of Isabella and her guardian angels. She had endured so much—losing her mother, living apart from ordinary mortals for hundreds of years. And she had returned to the world at such a brutal time, with heretics revolting against the authority of the Roman Catholic Church.

His thoughts spiraled away, and with a sigh he reined them in again, moving his finger to the next bead for another Ave Maria.

Thomas drifted into sleep as he prayed. When he came to with a start, the candles above the altar had dimmed. He rubbed his face and rose from his knees to sit on the wooden bench behind him. The walls of the underground room seemed to close in. He was uncomfortably aware of the weight of earth and rock above his head, and he remembered with a shudder the horror of his descent into the dark on the long stairway. Shadows filled the chapel, and in the dappled light the paintings appeared to shift and change. The eyes of the archangels glittered and blinked. They dipped their faces to one another, and their lips moved. Thomas pressed his palms against his eyes. The air smelled sweet, of frankincense and rose petals, above the older, earthier smell of cold stone.

"Father in Heaven, what is happening?" he whispered. He took his hands from his face and looked again.

The empty archway painted on the chapel wall was glowing. Suddenly, a sword of light slashed through the wall. The beam broadened, stretched, poured through the gap, too bright to bear. Thomas shaded his eyes, his mind full of clamor, fear, and excitement.

Isabella stepped through the opening in the wall—and saw Thomas sitting by the altar in the underground chapel.

He rose quickly to his feet. "Isabella, is it you?" he whispered.

She nodded. "Thomas, I need you to help me," she said. "Then we can take you away from here to a place where you will be safe." She placed her hand on his arm and felt him tremble. She knew the priest was accustomed to being strong and brave—he relied upon it. Now she was asking him to trust her, as a child would trust a parent.

He took a steadying breath. "I will do whatever I can," he said humbly. "To the very end of my life, I will help you, Isabella."

She gestured to the wall, to her picture. "Do you know who I am?" she asked. "Do you understand?"

Thomas nodded, keeping his eyes on her face. "I read about you," he said. "Jerome wrote of you and your life with the angels. He also recorded what he discovered of your mother's trial."

Isabella pulled away. "I wasn't brave enough to go to the trial," she said bitterly. "I couldn't bear it. I ran away. I left her alone."

"You did what you could. You were but a child," Thomas said. Then his thoughts seemed to turn, for he asked, "Do you know how Elizabeth fares? Is she safe?"

"She *will* be safe," Isabella replied. "But there's something we must do first. Then all will be well."

"Tell me," he said. "What must we do?"

Isabella sat on one of the benches, and Thomas dropped down beside her. She took a deep breath, gathering her thoughts. The priest had read the account written by Jerome and now, like him, believed the crow people were angels. And perhaps they *were* angels—God's messengers. Perhaps all the angels seen throughout the ages were truly from the shadow land, and like mirrors, they reflected what the people made of dirt wished to see: heavenly creatures or evil spirits. If she was to save Elizabeth and the rest of the Dyer family—and Thomas himself—it was important that he continue in this belief. But she realized that what she was about to ask of him might challenge his faith.

"My brother's bones are hidden here," she said. "I have to find them—and burn them."

The priest narrowed his eyes. "Why do you have to burn bones?" he asked.

Isabella sighed. "I can't explain," she said. "But it is necessary. Will you trust me? Will you have faith? You said . . . you said you would help me to the end of your life."

"I did," the priest admitted. "To the end of my life, but not to the peril of my soul. The burning of remains . . . it smacks of—" He pulled up short.

"Witchcraft?" Isabella finished, in a low voice.

"I'm sorry," Thomas said. "Can't you tell me why it is necessary?"

Isabella slowly shook her head.

The priest paled, and a sweat broke out on his forehead. He crossed himself and crossed himself again. Then he seemed to come to a decision. "I do have faith in you," he said. "Forgive my doubt. Where are they? Where are the bones?"

Inside, Isabella rejoiced, but she was careful to keep her demeanor calm. "Jerome promised me they would be sealed into a reliquary and preserved forever—here in the chapel of the archangels," she said.

"A reliquary? There is none here. None I've seen."

Isabella's heart sank. "There must be," she said. She rose to her feet and circled the tiny chapel. "It's here. I know it," she said.

"If you're right, there is only one place it can be," Thomas said. He rose and stood before the altar. He made the sign of the cross. Then he folded back the cloth.

Isabella went to stand beside him. The altar was a large stone box, covered in weathered carvings, with a huge limestone slab for a lid. She ran her fingers over the cold, pale surface.

"It will be heavy," Thomas warned. "Are you sure this is what must be done?"

"Yes," Isabella said. "See if you can push it aside."

Thomas walked from one end of the altar to the other, trying to decide the best way to approach the task. "Stand back," he said.

Isabella moved away to watch. The priest was a big man and well built, but even so, the slab was enormous. *Be strong enough,* she urged silently. *Be strong enough, Thomas Montford.*

The priest leaned forward, pressed his hands to the side of the slab, and brought his weight to bear upon it. His face reddened with the effort. His body contracted and heaved. But the lid didn't move.

"Please. Please try again," Isabella begged.

Thomas shook his head. "I am weak from lack of food," he said, but he did as he was asked. He moved to the other side of the altar and began to push again. Beads of sweat popped from his forehead. He let out a roar that filled the tiny chapel—and at last, the heavy lid shifted. The noise was terrible, the agonized grating of stone against rough stone. When Thomas's strength gave out, the lid was still upon the altar, but it was skewed to one side. A cloud of ancient dust rose from the opening he had created.

Isabella ran forward. "Is it there?" she asked anxiously. "Can you see it?"

The priest lifted one of the perpetual candles from the shelf and lowered it to the black mouth, shining the light into the hollow body of the altar.

Isabella strained to see. Candlelight glinted on some reflective surface.

Thomas stood up again, handed her the candle, then tipped himself over the stone lip to reach inside.

"What is it? Can you get it?" Isabella was impatient now.

"I have it," Thomas said. Carefully he rose. In his hands he held a dusty wooden box, finely carved and inlaid with gold. He maneuvered it past the lid and placed it on the ground. Using his sleeve, he wiped the dust from the glass top. "It's inscribed," he said.

"What does it say?"

"It's a name, Isabella. It says John Leland."

Isabella almost snatched the box away from him. She peered through the occluded surface into the reliquary. Normally, a saint's bones would be stored in a box such as this, so that the faithful might receive a blessing from the holy one. Jerome had kept his promise and locked away John's earthly remains in a place they would never be discovered, in the altar in the secret chapel underneath the hill. She cradled the box and closed her eyes, wondering if she might sense something of her brother in the bundle of dry bones. While these relics existed, Beloved of the Queen was not entirely one of the crow people. For as long as she held the bones, he was also her brother, John—a child made of dirt as she was— and she still had a claim on him. She embraced the box and shut her eyes, remembering the baby boy she had loved and cared for so very long ago. Could she let him go now? Apart from her mother, there was no one she had loved more. John was the last member of the Leland family . . . her only relative.

Isabella sighed. The little boy she had cuddled and fed and adored was long gone. The man he had become was someone very different. He had his own family and his own world. She had longed to bring him out of the shadow land to be her brother again, but she knew too well how little he would want the life she offered.

She closed her eyes. "I love you, John," she whispered to the bones in the box. "Even when you're truly one of the crow people, I will still love you." She felt a searing pain in her heart at giving him up. But John had been lost to her since the moment the Faerie Queen had lifted him from her arms.

Isabella opened her eyes. The priest was staring at her. His expression was concerned but kind.

"Are you certain this is the right thing to do?" he asked.

Isabella nodded.

They carried the box to an empty chamber and, by the light of the floating orb, built a small pyre using pieces of broken furniture and strips of old cloth. Isabella smashed the reliquary glass and tipped out five long bones. She gently placed them on top of the wood. "Go ahead," she said. "Light the fire now."

The priest had a flint, but he was doubtful the unlikely pile of kindling would light. He looked at her and nodded. "I'll try."

He crouched beside the pyre and sent a spark spinning into it. The spark hissed, and a small finger of smoke rose. The next instant, the entire heap was ablaze. The fire gave off a brilliant golden light but little smoke.

The priest stepped back. "It isn't an ordinary fire, to burn so fast and bright," he observed.

Isabella watched, spellbound, as the bones ignited and strange green flames danced over them. She felt as though a long thread tightly wound around her heart were slowly coming undone.

Within minutes the fire was utterly burned out. Everything was consumed—cloth, wood, and bones. Only a very fine ash remained.

Isabella sighed. She felt tired and empty.

As Thomas watched the flames, his misgivings melted away. There was a rightness to the deed, even though he didn't understand exactly what they were doing or why. He wondered what Isabella was thinking about as she stared into the fire. He could see emotions flickering across her face—grief and loss and also release. She would tell him if she needed to. He trusted her.

"Are we done now?" he asked quietly.

Isabella nodded, and they left the chamber and returned to the chapel, the light orb floating before them.

"When you and Elizabeth are together again, when her father is home, ask him to examine the records of your mother's trial," Thomas told Isabella. "I think you will be surprised. She was not alone and friendless, as you seem to believe."

Isabella turned to him quickly. "What do you mean?" she said.

Thomas didn't answer, for something was moving in the chapel—a tall, dark figure. "What is it?" he whispered.

"It's an angel," Isabella said simply. "He has come for us."

It was as if one of the paintings had stepped from the wall. The angel was beautiful, with great black wings like a cloak and hair like a crow's feathers. He seemed to blaze with unearthly glory.

Thomas dropped to his knees, and a sob left his lips. He was overwhelmed with gratitude for the vision. He raised his eyes to the angel and beheld a long white hand held out to him. Thomas rose to his feet and offered his own flawed mortal hand in return. The angel didn't speak. Its hand was smooth and cool, like a piece of marble.

Isabella ran across the chapel and jumped through the opening in the wall, disappearing into the light. Thomas and the angel followed her—and the world fell away behind them . . . chapel, library, town, earth, faith, life. For a moment Thomas was wiped clean. Everything was gone. He soared up to the heavens, to the palaces of God's light, and his mind was full of music.

25

Letters

lizabeth blinked. Merrivale's dagger was still hanging in the air, moving slowly, slowly, toward Isabella's chest. The days and years she had spent in the shadow land seemed to swirl away, shrinking and diminishing. How long had she been gone? A fraction of a moment, judging by the progress of the knife.

The faerie, John's father, had brought them back to the house in the wink of an eye. The tableau was just as they had left it: the clay cup in the air . . . Jane at the doorway . . . Merrivale with his hand outstretched, having released the deadly blade. Elizabeth was frozen to the spot, but as she watched, the faerie picked up the papers strewn over the floor—documents linking Thomas Montford and Robert Dyer in a conspiracy. He ran his fingers over the writing, and the letters swarmed over the page like ants before settling in new configurations. Then he dropped the pages and turned to stare at Merrivale. The faerie's face shifted. A cruel beak emerged, and his eyes became round, the yellow pupils slotted with black. Talons stretched from his fingers, and the feathered cloak shaped itself into two vast wings. Perhaps Merrivale could see what was happening, too, because his eyes widened with horror as the faerie knocked the dagger away, seized him by the ankle, and dragged him out the window.

Merrivale screamed. The knife hit the floorboards with a clatter. The clay cup fell to the ground and smashed. Smoke billowed into the room from the fireplace. All of a sudden the room was full of noise and commotion.

Jane ran in. "Are you all right?" she cried. "I thought Isabella would be killed."

Merrivale's men looked around the room in bewilderment. The goblins had vanished—and so had Merrivale. In a moment the situation had utterly changed, and they didn't know what to do.

Jane hugged both girls to her. "What happened?" she whispered to them. "Where has Merrivale gone?"

"I don't know," Elizabeth whispered back. "But I don't think he'll return. Isabella has made sure that we are safe from him—and that Thomas is, too."

Jane nodded. She stood straight, pushed the hair from her face, and became—as once she had been—the proud wife of a prosperous and distinguished Maumesbury merchant. She looked with scorn at Merrivale's men. "Where is your master?" she demanded. "I wish to speak to my accuser."

The men shifted about uneasily.

"I heard him scream," one of them said. "Then he disappeared."

"Where did the creatures go? The goblins?" asked another.

The third made the sign against the evil eye. They looked

at Jane suspiciously, as though they thought she might be the cause of the unnatural visitation.

"I see no goblins," Jane said coldly. "Why have you dragged my daughter here? I demand we be released and returned to our home."

Elizabeth's heart soared. Her mother was strong again, the months of weeping and self-pity falling away at this time of need.

Two of the men were still at a loss, confused by the fight with the goblins and uncertain how to proceed without Merrivale. But the third—the young man who had been in thrall to the goblin—took upon himself the mantle of leadership.

"Catholic witch," he said. "You're here to face charges of treason."

Jane stood firm. "Where is your evidence?" she said. "Show it to me."

The young man gave a cruel smile. He was regaining confidence now, clearly pleased with his newfound authority. He nodded to one of his fellows, who picked up the papers strewn on the floor.

Elizabeth stepped forward. "What do the documents say?" she asked.

"You know very well what they say," he replied. "They tell how your brother, Robert Dyer, was helping a Catholic priest—a traitor and heretic."

"Read them to me," Elizabeth demanded. "Read me the evidence."

The young man snorted. He grabbed the papers and began reading. But his derisive grin soon faded. He dropped the first page and turned to the next. Then quickly he flicked through the rest before throwing them to the floor. "Where are the real letters?" he snarled at the other men. "These are the wrong ones."

Jane looked bewildered, and Elizabeth touched her mother's arm, trying to reassure her.

The men shouted at each other now, searching the room, trying to find what they needed.

Elizabeth picked up one of the pages—and had to clap her hand over her mouth to stifle a laugh. It held fragments of a story, a folk tale about a faerie prince and a changeling.

Jane took the paper from her daughter. She glanced at the words and then shouted out above the argument of the men. "This is nothing but nonsense! You have no evidence, no reason to hold us. You are acting above the law. My husband will hear of this, and he will inform the queen herself of this vile persecution of a woman and two helpless children. You must take us back to the town at once."

The men argued among themselves. The two who were afraid the goblins might return wanted to leave as quickly as possible. The third was more afraid of Merrivale and what he would say when he came back and discovered they had let the prisoners go.

Elizabeth put one arm around her mother and the other around Isabella. She was certain the men would release them.

And so it proved. The two overruled the one. There were four horses in the stables, and the men hurriedly saddled three. Fear was getting the better of them now. They mounted and galloped off, shouting and cursing each other—

and cursing Merrivale most of all. That left Merrivale's gray for Jane and the girls.

The journey home took many hours. They had only a vague idea of where they were, so Isabella guided them from her memories of the flight on the back of the crow prince. They took it in turns to ride. Despite the distance and their weariness, it was a joyous time for Elizabeth. The weight of fear had lifted. The threat had been taken away, and they were together.

Isabella told them the priest would be taken to the north of England, where he had said he would find shelter and protection. Jane did not question this any further—and neither did she ask about the goblins. Perhaps she didn't remember clearly. Perhaps she didn't wish to.

Elizabeth talked excitedly of how happy she would be at home with Esther, her parents, and Robert. She said Isabella would live with them, too, and all would be well again. Although the memories of the shadow land had receded, she felt as though her senses had been sharpened. The sky was of the brightest blue. The last scarlet berries blazed on the hawthorn bushes. The air was fresh and sweet with the scent of the previous day's rain. Everything was perfect and marvelous and miraculous.

Elizabeth chattered on, but she was very aware of Isabella's loss. Her friend had given up her brother in order to save Elizabeth and her family. This happy reunion would never have taken place without Isabella's courage, intelligence, and sacrifice. Of all the marvels Elizabeth had seen in the shadow land, the one that still burned in her mind was the image of Isabella's faerie self, the beautiful, shining creature she had seen in the plain of snow. That was who Isabella truly was.

When Jane rode the horse, Elizabeth took her friend's hand. "I know you've lost your brother," she said. "I understand it must hurt. But let me be your sister."

Isabella nodded. She turned away and wiped her eyes, but she squeezed Elizabeth's hand tightly.

Darkness was gathering when the three reached the edge of Maumesbury. Tired and filthy from the journey, they trudged up the cobbles to Silver Street. A single candle burned in the window, and a small face stared through the glass. Then the face disappeared. A moment later the front door opened.

"Mum!" Esther cried out. "Mum!"

Jane ran forward and swept up her daughter in her arms. "Esther," she said. "Oh, Esther. I thought I'd never see you again."

Mary scuttled to the door. "Merciful Father in Heaven!" she said. "Mistress, I was so afraid! They said Miss Elizabeth was taken as well, and I didn't know what to do! Now here you are—all safely returned home."

26

Home

errivale screamed till his throat was raw and his voice gave out. He was flying through a freezing darkness, dangling upside down beneath a giant crow. From time to time the monstrous bird cawed or shifted the grip of its lethal claws on his ankle. The bird wasn't careful of him, and Merrivale swung to and fro like a rag doll.

The crow cawed one more time, a triumphant, guttural cry, and let its clawed foot unfurl. Merrivale slipped free and plummeted down, down through miles of sky. His fall was so far and so spectacular, he had time to consider the eerie black forest sprawling beneath him and the veil of snow on the ground. He saw three ordinary crows flap away in alarm. Then, with terrifying speed, the earth rose to smash him to pieces. Merrivale closed his eyes. . . .

When he opened them, he was lying in the snow beneath the trees. He sat up, gasping. He was unhurt. How could this be? There was no time to think, for he heard a movement among the trees. He peered through the dark trunks. A gray shadow stirred. It was a wolf.

239

Merrivale's heart seemed to rise to his throat. Instinctively, he reached for his dagger, but of course it was gone. He looked around for a branch—anything with which to defend himself—but then realized the woods were alive with wolves. Six, eight, a dozen, maybe more. They edged closer, staring with cold, yellow eyes. How calm they looked, how sure of themselves, how certain of their meal. They were silent. It was Merrivale who growled, his mettle up now, infuriated by the wolves' confidence. Did they think he would lie down for them? No, he would fight, using his boots and fists and teeth if he had to.

The wolves began to circle, and Merrivale crouched, ready to fend off the attack. But suddenly something distracted the creatures. A long, melancholy note sounded through the snowy forest from far away. The wolves turned from Merrivale, considering the sound of the horn. The note came again, sad and resonant, weaving through the dense winter forest. Merrivale didn't wait to find out who the hunter might be. He seized the moment of the wolves' inattention to break the circle and flee.

Merrivale ran through the snow. Branches slapped his face. Roots seemed to reach up from the frozen soil to trip his feet. The horn was closer now, and Merrivale wondered if the hunters might save him. But there was something about the eerie notes snaking through the trees that made him doubt he would be helped. In fact, the prospect of the hunters frightened him more than the circle of wolves. He didn't know why—and hadn't the time to think about it. Despite the cold, a burning sweat broke out all over his body. A primeval terror rose like a fire in the pit of his stomach.

Puffing, struggling through the snow, Merrivale ran faster. He could hear the patter of the wolves' feet and the thunder of hooves. How could horsemen ride so fast through trees? Closer they came, and closer. Once, he stopped to look back, struggling for breath, and glimpsed the hunters riding toward him. The horses were black with red eyes, and mounted on their backs were horned men, devils with long dark hair and pointed white teeth. In their hands were spears decorated with feathers. Merrivale turned and ran again.

Soon they would have him. He was exhausted; his muscles were giving out, his heart thundering. He could hear the panting of the wolves, could smell their hot, meaty breath. Just one more step, just one more.

The lead wolf jumped at his back, and the weight of it knocked him to the ground. He screamed and rolled over, batting the beast away with his fists. Then they all were upon him—and the hunters, too.

"I am dead," Merrivale thought in that instant. "I am dead."

Thomas Montford had been walking a long, long time. His boots were worn through, his clothing was soiled and ragged, his face was dirty. How far he had traveled and where he had come from he didn't know. Dimly he recalled his name and the purpose of his journey. He felt as if he were waking from deep sleep or finding a path through the thickest fog. Only now were his thoughts—like the landscape— coming into focus. He had dreamed . . . what had he dreamed? The priest stopped, suddenly remembering. He had dreamed of angels. Fierce, beautiful angels with black wings. A smile played across his face. He began to murmur his prayers.

Up ahead a man was trimming a hazel tree, cutting back the branches to the stout stump. He looked up as Thomas approached.

"Can you tell me where this path will take me?" the priest asked, gesturing.

The man put his axe down and eyed the traveler. "My village is a mile ahead," he said. "And York is another ten miles beyond that."

Thomas smiled. The man spoke with the familiar accent of his childhood.

The man looked the priest up and down, perhaps noting his damaged clothes. "You've been a long time on the road," he said. "What is your name?"

The priest hesitated. His family name was well known in this part of the world. His brother owned half the county. "Montford," he said at last.

The man's eyes widened. He put his hand to his hat in a gesture of respect. Then he said: "Are you the brother that went to France?"

"I am."

The man nodded. He crossed himself and dropped to his knees. "Bless me, Father," he said.

Thomas raised his hand in a benediction above the man's head.

"Will you come to the village and baptize my daughter?" the man asked.

Thomas laid a hand on his shoulder. "You take a risk, inviting me to your home."

The man rose then. "You have friends here," he said. "There are places for you to stay, and there's much work for you to do."

Elizabeth sat on a stool in a garden full of flowers, stitching a hem on a fine piece of linen. She could hear Isabella and Esther laughing in the kitchen as they helped Mary bake bread and buns. The perfume of yeast and cinnamon combined pleasingly with the scent of lavender and honeysuckle from the garden.

How utterly delightful it was to be warm, she thought, allowing her needle to rest for a moment as she turned her face to the sun. Swifts wheeled above the rooftop and swooped over the garden. A large cat the color of marmalade jumped onto the garden wall, complementing the mellow color of the bricks. How lovely everything was. How perfect—if you had the eyes to see it. Ever since she'd returned from the shadow land, the ordinary world had glowed with a particular brightness, as though she were seeing it for the first time. It was something she tried hard to hold on to—this sense of new sight.

Her mother came out of the kitchen carrying a freshly baked bun. "This is for you," she said. "Are you hungry?"

"Thank you. It smells delicious," Elizabeth said. She folded the linen and carefully stowed it in her work box. Jane touched her lightly on the head and passed her the bun. Elizabeth cradled it in her hand, enjoying the warmth.

She studied her mother. It was hard to say precisely why Jane looked different now—but she did. The worry had faded from her face. Because of Merrivale's disappearance and the lack of evidence, no charges had been made against the Dyers. They were still held apart by the townspeople because of their faith, and they still struggled to make ends meet, but after their terrible adventure, their social standing and straitened circumstances didn't seem to matter so much.

They hadn't seen Robert again, but a letter had come from Spain telling them he was studying to join the Catholic priesthood. Jane was sad not to see him but achingly proud of his decision and grateful he was safe. And because they had so nearly lost everything, they were all very glad of each other—appreciative and gentle and eager to be happy. Besides, it was early summer, and the weather was fine. The light stretched deep into the evenings, and they had plenty of time to talk, play cards, sing, and pray together.

Jane returned to the house, and Elizabeth studied the golden bun in her hand. How lovely it looked. It was almost a shame to bite into it.

Distantly she heard a knock on the front door and wondered vaguely who it might be. Isabella had a number of callers now. She had an extraordinary knowledge of medicinal herbs and potions, and it hadn't taken long for news of her skills as a healer to travel around the town. People who had previously shunned the household were prepared to overlook the Dyers' faith because they wanted a remedy for toothache or had a broken bone that needed to be set. Even though she was not yet an adult, Isabella's abilities were unsurpassed in the town, and she possessed such inner strength and calm, her presence alone was enough to soothe women in the extremity of childbirth and children in the grip of agues and fevers.

Elizabeth never tired of Isabella's company. But she was aware that, even now, life was not easy for her friend. She suspected that Isabella thought often about her brother. And she knew that because Isabella had lived for so long on her own, the constraints of spending every day with a family—however kind—were sometimes too much to bear. Although the green mottling was wearing off Isabella's skin to reveal a more ordinary cream and pink color, she was still a wild creature at heart. Every now and then, she disappeared into the forest and spent days and nights on her own, moving among the trees and animals.

"Elizabeth! Elizabeth!" Esther called from the doorway. "Elizabeth—it's Father! He's home at last! Quick, come quickly!"

She disappeared back into the house, and Elizabeth jumped to her feet, dropping the bun. She picked up her skirts and ran inside. She heard her father before she saw him—his voice at once so familiar and so strange coming from the front room of the house.

"Esther—let me see you! How you've grown!"

For a moment Elizabeth hesitated. It was almost overwhelming to have him home again. They'd struggled without him for so long. Then she stepped through the doorway ... and there he was, her father, Edward. His hair had grown long, and the gray was more evident than she remembered. He looked older. Thinner.

Edward had his arm around Jane's waist, but he came forward when he saw his elder daughter. "Elizabeth," he said, his voice thick with emotion. "You've changed. How grown-up you've become."

"Was your trip a success?" Elizabeth asked in a small voice.

Edward smiled. "It was successful enough. But more important, I'm home again with my family, in the place we all belong."

Elizabeth looked at Isabella, who was standing a little apart from the reunited family. Did her father know about her?

Edward nodded, understanding her unspoken question. "Your mother wrote to me and told me of our new daughter," he said. "She is not as green as I imagined from the description—but she is even more beautiful and remarkable."

Still Elizabeth hesitated, almost afraid to let go of the vigilance she had carried since his departure.

Edward smiled again, more gently now. "Have you a greeting for your father?" he said quietly, holding out his arms.

Elizabeth blinked, and tears spilled down her cheeks. She ran forward and pressed herself against his chest.

Scarlet poppies floated above the ripe wheat. The sun was fierce and glorious on the high summer morning. Isabella strode along the dry white lane, kicking up dust. Soon the harvest would begin.

She carried a basket and was heading for the manor at Spirit Hill. Elizabeth still visited Lady Catherine twice a week to keep her company, and often Isabella went, too. Lady Catherine had been happy enough for Isabella to stay with the Dyer family—though she had sought a promise from Edward that they would not press the Catholic religion upon her.

Isabella and Elizabeth had given Edward a careful account of their adventures. They told him about the trial of Isabella's mother's three centuries before, how angels had taken her from her own time and become her guardians, and how Isabella had befriended Jerome at the shrine.

"And now the angels have brought her to us, so that we might care for her," Elizabeth said, and Isabella smiled.

Much later that night, Edward had made his way to the secret library and read the saint's account. He'd found further proof of their tale in the painting of Isabella with the angels on the wall of the chapel. "My forefather spoke on behalf of your mother," he told her afterward. "There is a lasting bond between our families. The histories of the Lelands and the Dyers are woven together."

Isabella was content to live with the Dyers. They had taken great care to make her welcome, and she was fond of them all. Still, from time to time sadness would sweep her up, and she would be overwhelmed by recollections of everything she had lost. She longed to see her brother, and she yearned for the mysteries of the shadow land. Then grief, like a black cloud, would fog her mind, and mortal life would seem small and petty, lacking in beauty and color. But these times passed. Her skin was hardly green anymore, and when she looked at herself in Lady Catherine's mirror, she was always taken aback to see how much she had come to resemble her mother.

She was a Leland still, a priestess by blood and training. She sensed the presence of the crow people in quiet places, and sometimes, from the corner of her eye, she would glimpse the flash of black feathers, the glint of ancient gold. One day she would visit the shadow land again.

When Isabella reached the manor, the chamberlain admitted her and escorted her to the workroom, where Elizabeth was grinding pigments in the stone bowl. The two girls were good companions to Lady Catherine, and she was teaching them to paint.

The lady stood before a fresh canvas. "Isabella!" she called. "How was your walk from the town? Did you bring herbs with you? The cook has terrible pains in her stomach. She has been moaning and groaning all morning. Will you talk with her?"

Isabella nodded. Lady Catherine was cheerful these days. Her husband was expected home within a week, and she'd told the girls that he had promised to take her back to court at the end of August. She had ordered a lavish new dress of embroidered silk for the occasion.

The studio smelled of linseed oil, but the windows were open, and the fragrant summer air drifted in. In the corner a portrait was displayed on an easel. Perhaps it was strange that Lady Catherine should still have a painting of Kit Merrivale, but he had never returned to claim it, and the picture was too remarkable to sell or lock away.

Kit Merrivale was a handsome man, it was true—though Lady Catherine had captured the cruelty hidden behind the pleasing proportions of his face. Yet the picture had changed. In fact, day by day it altered subtly. Sometimes Merrivale looked terrified . . . sometimes sad and haunted . . . sometimes crazed or tortured with grief. And the background changed, too. Most often he was sitting before a landscape of snowy forests, but from time to time this became a great stone city or a range of barren mountains.

Oddly, Lady Catherine did not see these changes as clearly as the girls did. She marveled at the way the painting seemed to change moods, but she attributed this to her skill. Indeed, she reckoned the portrait was her greatest work and talked of taking it to the court—except that Merrivale's inexplicable disappearance had not made him popular with Queen Elizabeth and her advisors.

Some people speculated that he had been murdered by a rival faction in the queen's network of spies and informers. Others maintained he had taken her money and fled the country. Isabella and Elizabeth feared that another priest hunter might be sent to take up the work Merrivale had abandoned. But this had not happened. It was as if everyone had forgotten his mission and his accusations against the girls and the Dyer family.

Later in the day, after Isabella had brewed a purging tea for the cook's bad stomach, she left the manor and headed for the shrine in the forest. She and Elizabeth often tended the holy place together. Elizabeth prayed to the Virgin Mary and Saint Jerome, while Isabella remembered her mother and the crow people. They both treasured it because it was at the spring that they had first met.

The glade was full of sunshine and fresh green grass. Isabella sat beside the spring and washed her face and hands in the icy water. A fox trotted through the dappled shadows under the trees and across the glade. It showed no fear of Isabella and simply dropped its muzzle to the water for a drink.

In the last few weeks, another forest creature had called at the spring to drink. Less noble-looking than the fox, this beast was filthy and clumsy. Its teeth were black and broken, and its hair was unkempt. It wore ragged clothing and a single pearl earring.

Would it come today? Isabella wondered. She had the power to heal the creature, to bring it to its senses, and she was determined to win its trust. In her basket she had loaves of fresh bread, plums, and cheese.

She waited patiently until evening, but the creature never came. Perhaps it was wrestling with devils no one else could see or running from imaginary pursuers. Isabella sighed. She pitied the beast for its suffering and delusions. She hoped that one day, with her help, it would find a way out of the terrifying maze of its mind.

She left the food inside the remains of Jerome's cell and walked away from the shrine. Perhaps the creature, which had once been a man, would find the gift and enjoy the food. She would return soon with more.

Author's Note

In 1527, King Henry VIII of England asked Pope Clement VII, the leader of the Roman Catholic Church, to grant him a divorce because his wife, Catherine of Aragon, had not borne him a male heir. The pope refused, so Henry broke with the church and in 1534, through the Act of Supremacy, made himself the Head of the Church of England. In the 1530s, he closed down eight hundred monasteries across the country, taking over their land and property.

Henry's eldest daughter, Mary, became queen after his death, and she tried to restore the Roman Catholic faith in England. In 1554, a law was passed that allowed for the sentancing of Protestant "heretics" to death by burning. Almost three hundred people were burned alive during Mary's reign—with her full approval; she thus earned the nickname Bloody Mary. When she died in 1558, her younger half-sister, Elizabeth, was crowned queen, and England became Protestant once again.

In 1570, Elizabeth was excommunicated by Pope Pius V, who called upon loyal Catholics to remove her from the throne. English exile William Allen set up a seminary in Douai, France, to train missionary priests—ardent young men prepared to risk their lives to serve the Catholics in England. By 1580, more than one hundred such priests had come to England. Their presence and a number of plots, rebellions, and assassination plans by Catholic conspirators made the Queen suspicious of *all* Catholics.

In 1585, Parliament passed the Act for the Preservation of the Queen's Safety, which proclaimed that anyone knowingly receiving or aiding Catholic priests was guilty of a felony and that any native-born man ordained as a Catholic priest since Elizabeth's ascension could be convicted of treason. By 1603, approximately two hundred priests and ordinary Catholics had been executed.